love

at first

flight

Also by Christina Hill:

Love has a Name

To Love Again

love at first flight

A Romantic Comedy

Christina Hill

Copyright © 2022 Christina Hill

All rights reserved.

This book is a work of fiction. Any references to historical events, real people, or real places are used fictitiously. Other names, characters, places, and events are products of the author's imagination, and any resemblance to actual events or places or persons, living or dead, is entirely coincidental.

No part of this book may be reproduced, or stored in a retrieval system, or transmitted in any form or by any means, electronic, mechanical, photocopying, recording, or otherwise, without express written permission of the publisher.

Cover Design: Christina Hill

ISBN: 979-8-9857199-3-2

To Katie, my best friend and comedy inspiration.

To Samuel, my husband who laughs at my jokes.

CHAPTER ONE

Bryn

"Sir, excuse me, you dropped something," I say to the man in front of me. Bending to pick it up, I huff and mumble my irritations. We've been standing in this line for time only knows how long, and I'm over it. It twists and curves in so many places, I'm sure the end of it is somewhere outside in the drizzly Seattle rain.

I picked the wrong week to switch to homemade deodorant. My skin is still damp with sweat from my workout this morning. Who needs weights when you've got suitcases the size of a small vehicle to lift? I had to hoist those suckers onto one of the rentable carts I'm convinced the airport designed for me. I pushed them up to the counter with a shy look, because I knew they were over fifty pounds but I didn't know I'd be charged a small fortune to check them.

It'll all be worth it in the end.

Thank God my anxiety had me showing up at the airport four hours before my flight was actually set to leave. Someone in the "first time fliers" social media group recommended being here two hours before takeoff, so I doubled that time. I'd rather eat spaghetti with a spoon than be late to anything.

I stand upright again but the man still hasn't responded. Not a step, flinch, or any movement to speak of. I try again. "Excuse me."

Nothing.

Nada.

Zilch.

I huff and step to the side, noticing headphones in his ears. What's with people and their tiny headphones these days? Whatever happened to the large and in charge monstrosities that took over half your head and made it look as if you were broadcasting a football game? At least there wasn't any question if you were paying attention. I had a full blown conversation with someone in the meat department last week, or so I thought. It wasn't until they removed the plankton size headphones and asked, "Did you say something?" that I realized I was the only one complaining about the price of chicken—out loud—for a full two minutes.

I prefer to be alert. Prepared. Ready to take on whatever chaos is likely to proposition me. Maybe I've lived in the city for too long, or maybe I just prefer not to die with noise canceling headphones in. I can't say.

Tapping him on the shoulder, he extracts the small buds and pivots on his heel with a smile ready to slay hearts with a ninja sword.

I give him my best smile even if it's forced. "Here. You dropped your license."

It's then I discover my mistake. This isn't just any man standing in front of me. This is Zac Efron from High School Musical circa early 2000's with surfer hair falling in his eyes but on present day Zac's body. My mouth runs dry as I absorb the specimen in front of me. Anna, my best friend and sister, would be appalled that I just referred to an attractive man as a *specimen* but I think even she would understand.

His eyes are storm cloud gray. Nothing like Zac's, and I would know since his poster hung on my wall until I was nineteen. So what if I'm twenty-three now? I didn't even know eyes could be that color. They're mesmerizing. Dark around the edges with a piercing brightness surrounding his pupil. I want to dance in his thunderstorm if you know what I mean. His skin is the perfect shade of coffee with cream—the real kind, not the dairy free one. It's like he's been in the sun for days sans sunscreen. I would scold him for that, but his dark, disheveled hair and the five o'clock shadow makes me want to run my hand on, in, and through it.

"Oh." He reaches for his card.

I'm speechless, until I'm not. "Zac?"

"Huh?"

I shake my head. It was worth a shot. "Nothing. And you're welcome."

He stares. "Wait a sec...did I say thank you?"

My brain is clearly already on vacation mode. I think back on the few brief words we've shared and note that most of them were in my mind. A disbelieving laugh escapes my parted lips. *Okay, not Zac.* "Good thing I not only saved you from having to stand in line at the DMV for hours, but I single-handedly rescued you from being denied entry through this security line."

His blank stare persists as he rubs the underside of his jaw.

Did I just say all of that out loud?

"I was planning to say thank you, I just hadn't had the chance." He clears his throat, gesturing with his hand. "Thank you...for saving me."

I stand straighter. "You're welcome...again."

"Thanks...again." His voice wraps around my entire body like it's coating me in butter. Slick, smooth, and slippery. I'm practically swimming in a tub of it.

He tugs at his license that I haven't let go of. "I'm going to put it in my wallet now."

"Right. Sorry," I say, releasing it. Heat travels up my spine and wraps around my neck like a scarf.

He doesn't appear fazed at all. Not like me, who is precisely three seconds away from whipping out my blood pressure cuff to see if my heart, organs, and blood vessels are about to explode or not. It's a good thing I brought it.

It hasn't been that *long, Bryn. Get a grip.*

Finding the handle of my small carry-on suitcase, I grip it tightly and pretend not to steal glances at him every few seconds as he tucks his card safely back in his wallet.

He doesn't turn back around like I expect him to. I don't know what to do in situations like this with wildly attractive men. Not like it happens often or anything. I'd been in a long-term relationship for so long my eyes have apparently gone soft, finding random strangers in airports obscenely good looking to the point I'm daydreaming about them slathering me in butter.

Leaning on one leg, I peer around him, trying to gauge what's holding up the line from Hades and hoping Zac's twin will turn around and accost someone else with his tantalizing good looks. He doesn't.

"Rex." He extends a hand.

I stare down but don't make a move to grasp his hand. I've already run an initial analysis on his type and concluded he probably doesn't wear sunscreen, carelessly handles his driver's license, and wears headphones in public. Add to that the fact his name is *Rex*. It sounds like the name of a leather-wearing Harley rider. You'd get a tattoo of his name on your left butt cheek but wouldn't bring him home to meet your mom. No one named *Rex* is a good influence.

He drops his hand when I don't take it. "And you are?" he asks, drawing out the last word.

I've been avoiding his eyes. The ones that have the power to undress me on the spot. I've scanned the length of him twice already, and I refuse to make it a third time. But you better believe I noticed the flip flops he's wearing. Flip flops at the airport? Really?

My insides begin to tingle, and I worry that I've developed a foot fetish in the last five minutes. Shaking my head to get their image out of my mind, I reply, "Bryn," like I lost a bet. The last thing I want to do is pass the time chatting up a hot—and I mean sizzling—hunk of man at the airport considering the kind of day it's been. My nerves can't take much more.

I squeeze the handles of my purse that are slung over my shoulder in a tight fist, seeing red and nothing else.

"Are you okay?" he asks, facing me head on.

The line is at a standstill, like it has been for one million years. I don't get it. It hasn't so much as budged, but I keep throwing glances over his shoulder in case it does. It has to move. I have to make my flight in three hours, forty-three minutes, and ten seconds. WHY WON'T IT MOVE?!

I exhale. "Sorry. I'm a little on edge. This line is…" My voice trails off. Why am I apologizing? Because that's how things were with my ex, Jeremy. I miss the Bryn before Jeremy. The one that would loudly express her opinions in the middle of a movie without reservation. Or would slip on knee-high socks and drink box wine instead of wearing dresses she couldn't afford and tipping back drinks she couldn't pronounce. And the Bryn that was humble enough to know Jeremy could've been with anyone, yet cocky enough to believe he was the lucky one. Something changed for that Bryn though. She got lost. She changed.

Rage bubbles up inside of me, a cannon ready to burst. If I don't speak my mind, I'll be the same Bryn that dated a complete loser and believed he was royalty. I won't be that Bryn ever again. I promised myself.

"You know what? No. I'm more than on edge and I'm not sorry about it. I should have just gotten an InstantPot instead of coming on this vacation. I don't even know what a pressure cooker does or why they are better than a good old fashioned stovetop. Did you know there's going to be so much freaking sun where I'm going? I don't even like sun. I'd live in Seattle even if I wasn't born and raised here. My REI membership and pale skin are a testament to that. But my mother guilt tripped me into going even though I've never been on a plane before and never wanted to do this alone. And to top it all off, my sister had to stop for a dinner smoothie, because apparently that's a thing, and she promptly spilled it all over her front seat—with me in it—forcing me to pull out my designated day one outfit for a trip I begged my boss to let me take." I inhale deeply. "So no, I'm not okay."

I leave out the part that Rex is so annoyingly hot, he could probably have his own shirtless calendar. I can picture it now: an ax slung over his shoulder about to chop some wood—or someone's heart—for January. Him scaling a ten-foot tree to rescue a distressed kitten in nothing but low-rider jeans and cowboy boots for July. And don't forget December where he's dressed in a jingle-bell thong and Santa hat.

My thoughts have taken an unexpected turn.

He nods like he completely understands then his brows crease. "Wait. What's a *day one* outfit?"

My mouth hangs open as I continue to breathe deeply after venting to this perfectly acceptable stranger who is wearing a perfectly acceptable baseball cap—not a Santa hat. I can't believe I said that all out loud.

Oh God, I hope I didn't mention the calendar.

I shift my weight to my other foot, jutting out my hip. I'm in too deep. "A day one outfit simply refers to the outfit I picked to wear on the first day of my vacation." I flail a hand in front of my current ensemble: a black, sleeveless romper that stops mid-calf. "This is not a travel day outfit."

He holds up a hand. "Isn't day one the same as travel day?"

He has a lot to learn.

"Nooo. Day one is the first day of vacation. It's like chapter one of a book. Travel day is the prologue; it sets the stage for the whole book, but it has its own category entirely." I wave my hands frantically in front of me, talking right along with my mouth that won't shut up.

My sister, Anna, doesn't even know I plan out my outfits for each day of a trip, and she's supposed to know everything about me. If she knew, I'm sure she'd force me to take one of her weird online quizzes. The kind that determines your spirit animal —as if I didn't already know mine was an owl. The last one she sent me was to figure out which Disney princess I am most like. Ariel, because she has a strained relationship with her family and uses a fork to brush her hair.

I mean, the fork thing isn't really that relevant.

The line inches forward, and I gasp, pointing ahead. Rex peers over his shoulder and walks backward, his sandals flopping loudly on the linoleum tiles. He takes a wide stance when we stop moving again, trailing his gaze from my toes all the way back to my eyes. "Day one looks…good *and* comfortable."

I shudder, more out of irritation than desire. That's what I keep telling myself anyway.

CHAPTER TWO

Rex

I'm staring; I know that, but it can't be helped. This woman is beautiful. Not in the typical pretty woman way but more like the longer-I-stare-the-more-I-see-things-that-I-like way. That's why I can't stop staring. I'm afraid I'll miss something. Her rich brown hair and sharp green eyes are only second in line to her rosy cheeks and the pattern of freckles dotting her shoulders. I trace those with my eyes and let them fall lower.

I've scanned her full body thrice as we've been talking—scratch that—as she's been talking. Her mouth has been moving for the past five minutes, mostly ramblings, but I don't want to turn around. I want to keep staring. She's fascinating. I had no idea people chose outfits for specific days. I throw a handful of t-shirts, one pair of jeans, and all my underwear in a bag and call it good. I splurge on the amount of underwear I pack, because that's one thing you don't want to wear dirty. Call me bougie if you have to.

I smile brightly and cross my arms. "Couldn't you rewear an outfit?"

She scoffs. "No. I can't. What if I spill something? Or sweat? It's not like I can wash it easily. I'd have to go to a laundromat," she says, curling her lip and wrinkling her nose. "And I'd have to buy detergent, which is likely the cost of at least two margaritas."

I hold up both hands in surrender and take a step back as the line begins to move again. I could turn around and pretend like this conversation never happened. Like this beautiful woman isn't trying to sell me on the fact that day one, two, and three outfits are a thing. But I don't. I stay facing her, curious what she'll say next and how my body practically vibrates around her. I'm fairly confident I look like the heart-eyes emoji.

She doesn't get the chance, however, since airport security starts walking up and down the line yelling, "Please make sure all carry-on items are the proper size. Water bottles must be empty, and no sharp or hazardous items are allowed. We will have to confiscate them."

I don't think twice about the routine announcement. I've been traveling to Seattle from California to visit my mom every month for a year and a handful of times a year before my dad died.

Airports are familiar to me. But the way Bryn is now frantically searching through her oversized monster of a purse, she might as well have a neon sign indicating she's a first-time flier. I can smell her kind a mile away.

"Do you have something hazardous in there?" I tease. The look she shoots me could kill.

"I don't think I have anything…well, maybe…" She pulls out a small pair of scissors and now I'm convinced she has no clue what she's doing.

I quickly scan the area around us, making sure no one else is seeing what I'm seeing. "Don't hold those up so high. You can't bring those on the plane. Why do you even have scissors?" I whisper.

"Why are you whispering?" she whispers back before shrugging. "They're for my eyebrows, if you must know."

I stare blankly at her sea-green eyes and forget what's happening for a second. "Okay," I start, jumping into Mr. Fix It mode. "Do you have anything else sharp and pointy in your bags?" You know, like a pocket knife? Possibly a machete?

She glares at me. "No. Just scissors."

Just scissors. "Right. Well, I know you said you've never been to the airport before, but anything remotely resembling an implement of destruction— i.e. scissors—won't make it through security."

"What do I do with them now?" she asks, holding the scissors in an open palm. "I don't want to get kicked out."

The worry lines on her forehead are starting to worry me. "Look, it's okay. Here," I say, putting my hand out. "Hand them to me and I'll get rid of them."

Bryn's eyes widen, staring somewhere over my shoulder. "Security! Hurry!" She flings/tosses/catapults the scissors into my hand but her aim is atrocious and they fall.

And continue to fall until…

"Shit!" I yell way too loud. I fling my eyes wide when they slice through a thin layer of skin on the top of my foot.

She cups her mouth and stares down. "Oh my God. You're…You're bleeding."

I can't bring myself to look. I *hate* blood. The sight of it makes me squeamish and I turn into a pregnant woman with an aversion to eggs. "Is it bad?" I ask, then bite my fist. The first jolt of pain registers in my body, sounding the alarm that it's time to freak out. It's doubled down by the fact I don't get another response from Bryn, which makes me believe it truly is worse than I expected. A real bloodbath of horror brought on by eyebrow scissors.

I catch Bryn rifling through her purse. "I thought I had some bandaids…come on, where are you?"

Someone behind us gasps. "Sir, your foot!"

I nod, feeling faint as I break out in a sweat. "Mhm. Blood."

The ripples of concern travel from one nosey passenger to the next.

"Aha!" Bryn yells above the masses. "I don't have bandaids, but this will work better." Dropping her purse, she kneels down and it's the first time I allow myself to look.

I blink rapidly, afraid to put eyes on the gory mess that is now my foot, but it's nothing more than a small wound with equally small amounts of blood. But there is blood. Enough to give me double vision as my gaze flickers to the small package Bryn is peeling open. Is that a…?

"Pads can absorb more than bandaids," she says, as if that will bring comfort.

She dabs the top of my foot with the open feminine product and I'm not sure whether to be mortified or thankful.

Opening another thin package and tossing the wrapper aside, she rests it on top of my cut, tucking the ends under my foot. "There. That should hold." She mumbles something else not for my ears. But I heard everything.

"What was that about my shoes?" I cross my arms and prompt her as she searches for something else in her Mary Poppins bag.

She straightens and scowls at me briefly, the hint of a smile that was breaking her lip line now gone. "I said you should consider wearing real shoes next time."

I look down at my feet and back at her, pointing at my Rainbow brand flip flops that form perfectly to my foot giving me both comfort and proper arch support. "These are real shoes."

"Barely." She grips a small bottle and sprays her hands, rubbing furiously.

She beckons for me to put my hands out. I do, and she sprays my palms even though I never came close to touching any blood.

What smells like a mix of cinnamon and lemon invades my nose as I rub my hands vigorously. "Maybe you shouldn't bring scissors to an airport."

She slaps her thigh. "It was an accident!"

"An accident that could have sent me to the hospital for stitches," I say in protest.

"Oh stop. It's a small cut."

"I said, *could have*."

She rubs her forehead then lowers her voice. "I'm sorry."

I nod. I'm not upset, but the small amusement I read in her features is addictive. "Forgiven."

"Now could you scooch forward? The line is moving."

I shuffle with the rest of the line, doing my best to keep the pad from bailing off my foot. I hate to admit it, but it's actually a lot softer than I thought.

Which is more than I can say about the hard-edged woman I can't seem to look away from.

CHAPTER THREE

Bryn

Rex crosses his arms and I force my eyeballs to focus on something other than his neck muscles for a change. I sweep my gaze around the line of people in front and behind me and the frantic travelers nearly running up and down the halls. Apparently this is where you go if you need a workout.

"Since this isn't my first rodeo, maybe I could help you out. Teach you the ropes of the airport," he says, pulling my attention back.

I mirror him and cross my arms, cutting him a sharp look. "Like I need you to mansplain things to me."

He continues like this is an episode of Shark Tank and he has one shot to make his pitch. "Think of this like your Dojo and I'm your Sensei."

"I have no clue what you're talking about. I didn't play soccer."

His mouth falls open. "No, it's not—forget it. I only meant that I want to help. It can be hard doing something for the first time and having no cultural context whatsoever."

I put on my best Mark Cuban scowl and act like I'm considering his offer. He doesn't know that I've spent hours of my already busy life Googling everything there is to know about airports and planes. Weeknights and weekends posting questions on forums, printing out schedules, and laminating all of it like the Enneagram One personality type that I am.

But the scissors.

The scissors were an accident. Did I know sharp objects weren't allowed? Yes. Did I want to go a week without trimming my brows and risk them turning into fuzzy caterpillars that would morph into butterflies? No. Therefore, the clear answer was to bring them. But the scissor fiasco will go down in history with my photo printed next to it in textbooks. I can't have any more slip-ups like this one. I can't get kicked out. I need this vacation even if I keep telling myself that I don't. Bryn-before-Jeremy would have loved to travel, and Bryn-after-Jeremy *needs* to if only to prove she still exists.

"Fine. Deal." I stick out my hand.

He looks down at my offer and back at my stoic expression, then grips my hand with the strength of a hippo's jaw. "Deal."

I squeeze tighter as if we are moments from an arm-wrestling contest that I refuse to lose, because I will play dirty if I have to. But the glint in his eye tells me he will, too.

"LOOKS LIKE THEY'VE got the TSA dog out now. Line should move faster," Rex says over his shoulder, the very same one his backpack is slung over and makes him look even more like High School Musical Zac. He could break out into song and dance at any moment.

I push my rolling bag forward. I'm glad I'll be in my own air space soon and won't unnecessarily spill my guts to random strangers. The quicker I can get some chamomile tea in me before this red eye flight, the faster I'll be able to fall asleep on the plane.

Wait...Did he just say...

"Dog?" I say loudly.

He turns to face me again, drops his bag, unzips his hoodie, and peels it off his tree trunk arms that somehow fit in there. "Yeah. They bring the dog out every so often to help find any substances that people try to sneak through. It helps the line move faster."

I blink rapidly, momentarily stunned by the pull and flex of sculpted muscles chiseled into his body. It's not like his t-shirt is made of spandex and clinging everywhere but it's tight enough to create a mental picture. *This* was hiding under *that*?

I gulp and immediately start shaking my head. "No, no. I can't," I start to explain. "I don't like *dogs.*" I whisper the last word, hoping no one in our vicinity hears me. This opinion isn't widely accepted, especially in a city like Seattle. Dogs get birthday cakes and their own place settings at holiday dinners. I, on the other hand, would rather perform a choreographed dance routine in public than pet a dog. I'm terrified of them. *All* of them.

He stares blankly at me. "How does someone not like dogs?"

"I'm more of a cat person."

He scrunches his nose in disgust.

"Let me guess, you don't like cats?" I ask, though I'm not really asking.

He shakes his head vehemently. "Absolutely not."

I laugh. "So, you've never been to a Cat Cafe then?"

"What the deuce is that?"

I shoot glances around him as I explain. "You know, cafes where you can drink coffee, order a pastry, and snuggle some cats."

"I'm pretty sure you're describing Hell."

"Did you not hear me say coffee and pastries?"

He shakes his head. "No. I heard you say cats that will sprinkle hair in your food—*on purpose.*"

I know there's a story here, but I'm too distracted by the security guard and his burly German Shepherd to ask a follow up question. The size of its paws could rival a grizzly's, and the long snout jutting out from its face looks like a pointer finger aimed straight at me.

Rex follows my line of sight which is currently scanning the height, width, and length of the creature weaving in front and behind people, sniffing their luggage and rear ends.

I breathe in and out slowly, hyping myself up with a pep talk I didn't come prepared to give.

It's probably a nice dog, Bryn. Trained. Well-behaved. Sweet and cuddly when it's off the clock. Friendly, even. Don't worry about those beady eyes that glow or ears tuned to the screams of their victims.

The wilder-beast yawns, exposing fangs that could easily sink into flesh. *My* flesh. "Dear Lord, those are big teeth."

"Are you scared?" Rex asks in disbelief as if he can't possibly imagine why I wouldn't want to cuddle up to an alligator with fur.

"I'm not *scared*. I just prefer animals that are… smaller."

"The dog is just doing its job. It's not like it'll bite." Rex swings his gaze between me and the dog. "You've got nothing to hide anymore, right?" he asks, winking at me.

My heart is racing but I can't tell if it's the effect of Rex's wink or the wild animal with the super-sniffer about to make contact with my ass.

Rex is next. Security waves him forward, and the dog's ears stand upright as he slinks behind him, sniffing at his heels. This descendant of wolves moves past him with no more than an uninterested glance. Rex turns and pumps a fist in the air, giving me an encouraging morale boost.

I roll my eyes and smooth down any potential fly-aways on my head, though I know that's impossible with the product I use to glue every hair back into a sleek ponytail. But I need something to distract myself from this one-hundred-pound creature with confirmed fangs and hidden intentions.

I'm waved through, but I pause. My feet won't move.

"Ma'am. You can walk through now. Keep the line moving."

You can do this. Give this dog your cat-like energy.

I inhale deeply and roll my shoulders back, adopting an I-don't-give-two-effs posture, just like a cat would. I shove that fear aside and strut forward.

But the dog can somehow still smell my terror like it's a freshly butchered chicken leg ready to be devoured. I take no more than two steps before the wild animal becomes laser focused on me and…sits. That's right. The dog sits down like he's bored of sniffing me. Does he not like the citrus body oil I use? Possibly my homemade deodorant? What gives?

I'm met with the guard's flat palm in my face as I freeze. "Ma'am. We'll need to check your purse."

"What? But the dog." I point at the angelic animal staring attentively at the guard. "He's sitting and…and calm."

"Exactly," he says with a nod. "Follow me."

I gulp, remembering exactly what I forgot to take out and throw away. Reaching inside, I extract the small bag of brownies Anna slipped in before I got out of the car tonight. "Wait! It's probably just my brownies," I say with relief. "He must have smelled them."

This dog isn't even barking or whining or anything. He's blinking slowly, thinking about the treat he'll get after this for finding the trouble: *me*. The guard swings his gaze from the dog to my bag of brownies suspended in the air, lowering his brows with a distrustful glare. "We're going to need to test those."

It's at this very moment that I realize these may not be normal brownies.

They might be the special kind.

CHAPTER FOUR

Bryn

After a full bag search and equally complete pat down, I'm finally cleared by security to leave their special offices for hardened criminals. My long-winded explanation of *why* and *how* those brownies ended up in my bag was ignored. Saying, "my sister put them in my purse," is as bad as saying, "my dog ate my homework."

Tightening my hold on my carry-on handle, I drag it behind me, scolding it when it bends left when I'm clearly going right. I hike my purse further up my shoulder and walk to get a snack and trashy magazine with celebrities in compromising positions sprawled across the front cover. This feels like the thing to do. But I'm no more than a few steps through security when I notice the familiar shaggy hair and muscular shoulders I was admiring earlier in line.

Rex.

"Hi," he says, providing no further explanation as to why he's there. Waiting. For me.

I stop momentarily to stare at his stormy eyes. One. Last. Time. Then, I keep moving. "Um, hi." Heat circles my neck knowing he just witnessed one of my top five most embarrassing moments. Forget it, I can't think of any that were worse.

He follows me. "So, they let you out, huh?"

I glance over my shoulder. "Yup."

"Did you at least get to keep the brownies?"

"No. And they weren't mine. They were…" I gulp. My cheeks are on fire. "And no thanks to you. I thought you were supposed to be my Dojo?"

"Sensei?"

I walk faster. "What?"

"Nothing. Just watch The Karate Kid, it will explain everything." He matches his pace with mine. "Where are you headed?"

I keep my gaze trained forward. "Getting a snack and something to read."

He shoves his hands in his pockets, appearing unbothered by how fast my feet are moving. His legs are long though, taking one stride to my two.

"Cool, but I meant, where are you flying to?" he asks.

I stumble forward, tripping over my own snakeskin sneakers and nothing else when Rex juts out an arm to steady me at my elbow. My body burns at the brief contact, the fingers wrapped tightly and tickling the sensitive area on the inside of my arm. He doesn't linger, and I'm glad for it, but the damage of his touch has already been done. I roll my shoulders back and clear my throat. "Did you come up with that prying question on your own, or did you find it in '101 Creepy Stalker Questions?'"

"I wrote that book," he deadpans.

I cut him a look. The smile is already plastered on his face. "Are you always this attentive to random strangers you meet in the airport?" My tone is clipped but I can't help it when this day has been full-on disaster mode. *More like the last four months.*

"Never."

There is so much packed into his one-word response that I don't even know where to start. "Look, just tell me if you're trying to kidnap me. I'll save you the hassle."

He laughs so hard; he bends at the waist and grips his stomach. "Oh, that's rich. I'm not going to kidnap you at the airport. Where would I take you?"

I shift my weight to my other foot, crossing my arms.

I don't know, Rex, maybe the air duct near the C gates that's big enough to fit two people. Because I'm an architect, I was able to access floor plans of this place and studied them as if I'd be tested on every escape route.

"Do I look like a kidnapper?" he asks, waving a hand up and down his lean, toned body.

I can't help but stare. His physique is magnificent. I'm positive he might already have a sexy calendar out in the world. He cares for himself, his body, his lush hair curling over his ears thanks to the hat. And those dark brows and lashes only highlight the color of his eyes. It's irritating me. The t-shirt and jeans he's wearing are clean and free of wrinkles, thank God. I might have had to offer him my small travel iron. I push further. "Serial killer?"

He shakes his head.

"Okay, fine. You don't look like a kidnapper," I finally admit and rather painfully. "Or a serial killer."

He nods. "Good. Now that it's settled, can I buy you a drink?" His smile is pure honey and I want to drench myself in it, pour it over my head and let it trail down the length of my body. Forget the butter his voice rubs all over me. I like honey more.

Stop right now. These thoughts are reason enough to shoot him down. "No."

"Wait. Really? Do you always turn down a free drink?" he asks. "In fact, maybe you should buy me a drink." He tucks his hands in his back pockets and his t-shirt strains against his broad chest.

I scoff, annoyed by his muscles. "How do you figure?"

Wiggling his foot between us, I look down. *Ugh. The foot.* "You're still wearing the pad?"

"It's comfortable."

I bite the insides of my cheeks to keep from laughing. "It's late."

"It's one drink."

"It's not..." my words drop off.

He leans closer, attempting to catch my eyes.

I evade them like they have cooties.

Swinging my purse to my other shoulder, I huff. "It's not like me." After all the honesty I've offered him today, this is by far the most vulnerable. I don't even know where it came from; the words just hiked up my throat and tumbled out. Maybe I don't even care, because the way he catalogs my face, nods, and leans closer reads like a specific brand of acceptance—his brand. My breath lodges in my throat.

He slings a safety net between us and asks me to jump. "Does that make it impossible?" He straightens. "Or just different?"

I shrug. "Both?"

A lazy smile tips the corner of his mouth. "If you really aren't interested in a drink, I can respect that. I'll walk away and let you board your flight with the chainsaw I know you're packing in that roller bag. But if there is a part of you that's curious, I know a place."

For the record, I don't have a chainsaw in my suitcase. It isn't practical for this trip. And it's only one drink. I could use one for my nerves. It doesn't matter that those nerves have more to do with him than they do about flying.

"One drink. You buy."

"I'll buy."

"Good," I say.

"Great," he adds, needing to have the last word.

I don't let him have it. "And the pad…" We both look at his foot being hugged inappropriately. "It has to go."

He nods his agreement, and we start walking, this time I reluctantly follow him.

I'm not a one-night stand kind of girl, but this is exactly what our scenario equals; one night is the sum of our potential together.

Maybe one night is all I need.

CHAPTER FIVE

Rex

I've already missed my flight home to California. That was a given when I decided to wait for her outside the security office like a stalker—or a deeply interested party—to make sure she was okay. I planned to book another flight but something in this filtered airport air has me thinking up new ideas.

We get a seat at my favorite airport bar right away. Bar seating is preferable anyway. It isn't because we'll be sitting close together, though that thought did cross my mind. It's because bars ease the tension by giving our eyes something else to focus on. First dates can be awkward sitting across a table and staring into the other person's eyeballs. Not that this is a first date or anything.

It's busy here tonight. Though Jack's Bar and Grill usually is even early in the morning. When you're traveling, anything goes. Morning might as well be night and vice versa. The dinner rush is just getting started as one order bleeds into the next, creating a frenzied foot pattern for the bartender to keep up with.

"So, *Rex*, do your friends call you T-Rex?" She bites down on her lower lip to conceal a smile and now I'm greedy to see a full one on her perfect mouth.

"Only one," I say loudly above a blender.

"Oh yeah?"

"Yup. She's the kind of person that loves cute nicknames," I start to explain.

"Mhm." She crosses her arms and leans forward on the bar top, watching the swirl of activity.

I look at Bryn from the corner of my eye. "She's also the kind of gal that assigns outfits to specific days." I give in to the pull to turn my head and look at her.

Her brows scrunch together, and I want to press my thumb between them to smooth out the crease. "This friend of yours sounds practical. She must have a capsule wardrobe, too," she says.

I start nodding like a bobblehead. "She definitely has whatever that is."

A smile spreads across her face, and it's just as I remembered. Full rose-colored lips with a cupid's bow curve that I've traced with my eyes forty-seven times already. I lick my lips to keep from drooling.

Before either of us can respond, we're interrupted by a loud customer who approaches

Bryn's side of the bar. "No, I said I wanted a hazelnut latte, not too hot, with minimal foam, skim milk, and a dash of cinnamon."

The bartender stares blankly at this middle-aged woman bending closer, as if he didn't hear her. "This is a bar. We don't have—"

"Hazelnut. Not almond. I don't want my coffee to taste like nuts," she says, her voice raising an octave higher, teetering on soprano territory.

I lean closer to Bryn and whisper in her ear. "Does she know hazelnuts are nuts?" Her back is inches from my chest and I'm unable to resist her scent. How does she fit an apple orchard into her shampoo bottle? I'm frolicking in a field of fresh apples in the fall.

I only vaguely hear a disgruntled Koffee Krazed Karen in the background as I calculate the remaining distance between our bodies in the foreground. My breath moves the sleek hair I've been inhaling, and my knees bracket her chair, inching closer with every breath I don't take. What is it about this woman that makes me want to be this close? I'm losing my apples, quite literally. Bryn is nothing like me and nothing like my last girlfriend, Claire, who surfed, loved dogs, and had dreads. Even with so much in common though, it was never right with Claire. I finally had to break it off when it felt like I was talking to myself and not a different person.

It's minutes, no, seconds—I really have no clue how long—before Koffee Krazed Karen decides she's done ordering her coffee at a bar. The steam coming out of her ears and the flapping hand movements she's making causes me to lean further back as she storms past us. I'm afraid she'll decide to pounce like the wild animal she's channeling.

Bryn must have had the same idea, because now her back presses against my chest. I feel every place our bodies connect. The hand she unknowingly uses to grip my knee, her bare, freckled shoulders that make my body temperature rise ten degrees, and her head tucked neatly under my chin. She fits. I don't know why this information shocks me, but it does.

With Koffee Krazed Karen gone, Bryn immediately peels herself off of me. "Sorry. That was…"

"Uncalled for? Crazy? Confusing?" I supply.

"All of those things." She pivots in her chair to face the bar again. I slowly and reluctantly do the same, pulling my knees back to my side.

I clear my throat as the bartender approaches us. "What can I get you two?" he asks.

"Rum and Coke," Bryn says without skipping a beat.

"No latte for you?" I ask and pull a small laugh from Bryn and the bartender. "I'll take a Spacedust IPA. Thanks." I rub my hands along the tops of my thighs. "So, uh, now that you know I'm not the craziest person in this airport," I point in the direction Karen just left, "do I get to know where you're flying?"

"Florida," she replies with a smirk.

"That explains the sun."

She shoots me a questioning glance.

"Earlier, in line, you said you didn't like the sun. Florida does have a lot of that," I say.

"Yeah, so I've heard. Plenty of Vitamin D and all that, my Mom tells me." She rests her chin on her propped elbow, staring at the mirror behind the shelves of half-full bottles of all shapes and sizes.

"Are you close to your mom?" I ask.

"Yes. And no."

I rest my forearms on the bar top. "That sounds complicated."

"It is," she says with a slight shake of her head. "I'm adopted. My mom never made me feel any different than my older sister and I love her for that. But it's no surprise how different I am. If I hadn't grown up knowing I was adopted, I'd for sure question it now. I don't know my biological parents though so who knows if I'm anything like them either."

Her voice sounds sad, which makes me sad for her. "And your dad? Are you anything like him?" I press.

"A little. We both loved music. I went to my first concert with him. He was the worst dancer but the most committed," she says with a small smile. Her voice becomes strained as she traces the wood grain of the bar top with her pointer finger. "He died when I was sixteen."

A familiar ache fills my chest at the memories of my own father. "I lost my dad a couple of years ago." I don't expand on the statement but I'm not shriveling up and hiding either. Progress.

She leans her head further into her palm and looks over at me. I stare back, caught in the forcefield that's been created through our similar experiences. I know what losing a dad has been like for me, especially since we were so close.

I open my mouth to thank her for sharing a part of herself when the bartender returns with our drinks. He sets them in front of us and we grasp for our glasses. I take a sip and consider the only thought that keeps running through my head. With every word this woman says, I like her more. I'm intrigued. She makes me more curious than any other woman I've met in a long time. And if my dad were still here, he'd tell me to keep my eyes open for people that were worth risking it all for. I don't have much but maybe that's all I need. I watch Bryn take a sip and wonder if I can risk like he did. He said my Mom was way out of his league but wouldn't decide that for her. Ultimately, she chose him, too. Yet, I'm not my dad. I don't know if I can be like him, but I want to.

I take a long, slow pull of my beer then set it down, wiping at the condensation. "You said you're going to Florida?"

She stirs her rum and Coke with the small straw, the ice clinking against the sides becoming the loudest sound in my ears. "Yup. I'll be posted up on some Miami beach with a Piña Colada in one hand and a book in the other."

I swallow. *You can do this, Rex. You can risk.*

Turning to face her, I bark out a sudden and way too exuberant laugh that makes her jostle her drink. "You're kidding?"

She snorts and mops up a small spill on the bar top. "Out of all the things I've told you today, you think that's a joke?"

"No, I mean," I scratch at my jaw. "I'm going to Miami, too." *Once I change my ticket,* I fail to add.

Her smile falls, which is saying something since she wasn't smiling. "Are you serious?"

"Dead serious," I say and regret it once the words are out. I'm really not helping change this creepy stranger vibe she's pinned me with. I shake my head. "Yeah, I'm going to Florida. Looks like we'll be able to continue your airport lessons."

"Hm," is all she says.

We are the picture of opposites. I'm smiling, she's frowning. I'm leaning forward, she's leaning back. I'm about to high five her, she's about to fake an illness.

Straightening, she lifts her glass. "Um, cheers. I guess."

I raise mine. "To Miami"

"To Miami," she says, and then downs the rest of her drink.

CHAPTER SIX

Bryn

As we walk to N9, *our* gate, every sound becomes louder. My senses are heightened, and I'm now acting like an animal in heat or something since my mind is laser focused on the feel of Rex's chest still lingering on my back. I didn't mean to lean that far when that woman decided to morph into the Black Friday version of herself that didn't get the discount on slippers she wanted. But it happened, and I can still feel the heat etched into my skin, his breath hot on my neck, my hand sizzling as it rested on his knee.

My brain turned into flubber, which is a substance I'm not even sure is real. Rex. Hot. Man. Touching. Me. Words are hard when he sucks up all of the air I'm trying to breathe and replaces it with some kind of juju magic that forces me to find him charming. Well, he's not *that* charming, okay. So, ha.

My footfall verges on stomping. Sure, he has a hot-guy aura for days, but that doesn't mean anything. We're just two people going to the same place. What is it about airports that makes it feel like you could find your one true love? Is it the lighting? Something in the air? It's gotta be the water. Love is definitely not what's happening here. We may both be going to Florida, but that still means nothing. I live in Seattle and he lives…well, he lives somewhere that has branded the smell of salt water into his clothing and tanned his skin to golden perfection. It's not like this will go anywhere. I'm fragile. Aren't I? Jeremy and I broke up only four months ago.

Four lonely months.

I swallow the lump in my throat that likes to appear whenever I think about Jeremy. He broke my heart and then acted like he could fix it. Sorry, pal, not gonna happen. It killed me to have to cancel our wedding venue and forfeit the deposit. The only thing worse was missing our cake tasting appointment. I had dreams of red velvet cake with buttercream frosting taunting me for weeks after that. I'm glad I found those texts revealing that he'd been cheating. If I hadn't confronted him, if I ignored all of the warning signs, and if I ate red velvet cake then somehow I'd be sealing my fate. I would have married someone and lost even more of myself than I already had.

That's why I need this vacation. I want to be okay just being *me*. No more pretending to be someone I'm not. If a man can't like me—quirks and all—then I won't like him. Although, to be clear, my quirks are few.

My phone scream-vibrates at me from inside my purse. I stop and fumble around for it, bypassing lip-gloss, my label maker that I never leave home without, and a small sewing kit that the security guard somehow didn't confiscate.

I cradle the phone between my cheek and shoulder. "Hello?"

"Bryn, I've been texting you."

"Anna, hi." I slide my gaze from Rex back to my purse, giving it a good shake as I grab my roller suitcase and continue walking.

"Why did you just give me your fake *hi*?"

I stutter. "Um, because, I—" I swivel my head away from Rex and lower my tone. "I'm at the airport."

"I know. I dropped you off, remember? Are you feeling okay? Did you already get into the *snack* I packed for you?"

"What? No. Though remind me to yell at you for the weed brownies later," I grind out. "No, I'm with…" I look over at Rex to make sure he isn't listening. He's not, but I get distracted by the carvings in his arms highlighting biceps. Were those there before? Or did he just grow those from walking? "I'm with…"

"With who?" she asks then gasps into my ear. "OH MY FRUITCAKES, DO YOU NEED ME TO CALL 911? Are you in trouble? Blink twice if you need me to call." Panic spews from her mouth. "No, wait. Don't blink. I can't see you. Cough! That's it, cough once and I'll hang up and call the cops."

I don't cough or blink. "I'm fine." Lowering my voice even more, I cup the hand holding the phone and speak slowly, without panic, into Anna's ear canal. "I'm walking with a guy right now."

The gasp that comes out of Anna's mouth is louder than the one she made when she thought I was in trouble. "You are not." Statement. Fact. No room to dispute.

But I do anyway, because we're sisters. "Yes, I am. We just met. I'll tell you about everything later."

"Journal every detail. Do not leave anything out. Including the bathroom make-out sesh."

It's my turn to gasp. "Anna, ew. Do you know me at all?"

"I thought I did until you told me you are walking with a strange man you don't know out of your own free will." She has me pegged, I'll give her that. "Okay, I really can't wait. Tell me everything before you hang up and go have wild—"

"Not happening," I interject.

"Is he hot? Give me a number between one and ten," she asks—no, *begs*.

I grip my suitcase handle tighter and delay responding. I know the number. I've known it since

Rex turned around in line and stared blankly like I was a wooly mammoth coming to trample him. But I'm annoyed that he's going to get that number from me. That he's earned that right from my eyeballs and there's nothing I can do about it. At least he doesn't know.

She won't rest until she gets a number. I sigh loudly into the phone, drawing it out for at least five seconds. "Ten."

She screams and I pull the phone away from my ear. "YOU ARE TOTALLY MAKING OUT WITH—"

"No!" I cut her off. "You're wrong. Again, do you know me at all?" I'm yell-whispering into the phone but it's no match for her actual yelling.

Stepping onto the escalator that will take us down to the underground trains, which Rex told me we would have to ride in order to get to our gate, I hold the phone away from my ear and let Anna finish freaking out. I stare in front of me at the backwards hat on Rex's head. I repeat, he's wearing it *backwards*, and now I'm rethinking the number I gave him. He's not a ten…he's an eleventeen-thousand, which isn't even a real number. But he has his own number scale.

Rex turns to look at me. "Next train will be here in three minutes."

I relax knowing he wasn't about to confront me to say he heard every single word of my conversation with Anna or myself. "Great," I say as we both step off the escalator.

"Ooo, is that him? He even sounds like a ten."

"Anna..." I add a slice of warning to my voice.

"Snap a picture of him when he's not looking and send it to me."

"No way, that's...that's weird."

"No it isn't! If he catches you tell him your sister needs proof he's not a murderer."

I pace in front of the sliding doors that will lead to the train when it arrives. "I've already confirmed that's not the case."

"Tell him you're a photographer for sexy calendars." I roll my eyes. It's like she's in my brain.

"I have to go, Anna."

"WAIT!"

"What?" I ask.

She lets out a breath. "This is a big, monumental, and very important moment."

I give a clipped laugh. "How do you figure?"

"Because this is the first guy you've come remotely close to considering a ten since *you know who* cheated and crumpled your heart like a cracker. Maybe you're not destined to be together forever with this ten, but there's nothing wrong with enjoying his company...or making out."

My smile softens at her words. She's right. Well, everything but the making out part. "Thank you, Anna."

"Of course. I mean, come on, you won't even admit Channing Tatum is a ten! This is a BIG deal."

I don't bother whispering. "Tatum isn't my type."

But Zac Efron is.

"Don't forget to take his picture and send it to me. Oh, and the journal! Write down everything!" she exclaims.

"I'm hanging up now." I tap the red button on my phone screen before she can say anything else. Walking back to where Rex stands stationary, I give him a timid smile. "Sorry, that was uh…" I have no words. I'm still tasting the flavor of admitting who Rex is to my sister. He is a fully formed ten in her brain now and I will never hear the end of it. And the baseball hat is doing a fine job at scrambling my thoughts. "My sister."

"The one who stashed the spiked brownies in your bag?" he asks with a wink.

"The very same one."

He smiles and the curve of his lips makes me forget my own name, let alone my sister's.

CHAPTER SEVEN

Rex

The train arrives and the sliding doors open and release a horde of focused travelers intent on a destination that isn't here. We do our best to dodge the blood-sucking piranhas dragging suitcases behind them while swimming upstream. Add in the small devices pressed close to their ears and our attempts at passing these reckless swimmers without bruises to show for it are futile.

"Grab my hand," I say to Bryn, who is a few steps behind me.

"I can't! You're too far!"

I look between the sliding doors and Bryn's distressed expression then swim back to her. The recorded voice comes on over the loudspeakers, drowning everything else out.

"Doors closing in ten seconds. Stay clear."

The reminder beats hard against my skull. I'm no longer in an airport. I'm a quarterback and it's fourth and goal from the two yard line with seconds left in a tied game. I'm calling an audible. All eyes are on me. Will I make the play?

Absolutely, I will.

I stretch and reach for Bryn's hand. She squeals but I grip tighter. The crush of people are now heading in the same direction as us, through the sliding doors, and into the waiting train.

"I can't keep up!" Bryn yells from behind, her hand slipping. "My suitcase!"

Her bag has a bum wheel, an injury we don't have time for.

"We're out of time outs. We have to go for it!" I yell back to her. My feet keep moving, driving forward through inside and outside linebackers, a defensive tackle, and who's this? The nose guard? Not on my watch. I drop Bryn's hand and spin in almost a full circle, evading Businessman Brent who thinks he can use his briefcase to block. Guess again, sucka.

I almost scream "throw the flag" and let the officials deal with him when the recorded voice sounds again but this time with a ding indicating the seconds we have left on the countdown clock.

Five…four…three…

I whip around and grasp Bryn by the waist, tugging her forward as I drive back into the waiting train car.

Two…one.

The doors close and the noise in the stadium quiets. I open my eyes, with no recollection of closing them, and look down at Bryn flat against my chest, breathing heavily.

We did it, we won the game.

The adrenaline high begins to wane and Bryn, seeing that she is saran wrapped to my body, stands upright quickly, brushing imaginary hairs away from her face. "Is the train always like this?"

A smile grows across my face, and I shrug. "Yeah, pretty much."

The train starts moving and Bryn, who isn't holding onto a pole, loses her balance and begins to go down sideways. I have reflexes like a cat, despite hating them, and grab hold of her waist again, drawing her closer. One of her legs coils around mine like a snake attempting to squeeze the life out of me while her arms tighten around my core, pinning my arms to my side.

I'm still holding onto her waist, one hand splayed across her lower back and the other on her much lower back.

This went better than I expected.

When the movement of the train no longer threatens her balance, she unravels herself from me and grips the pole instead. A red hue climbs her neck and settles on her cheeks, making me smile. I want to rub my knuckles across her skin to see if it feels warm, too.

She clears her throat and bends down to pick up her suitcase that had toppled over like Bryn almost had. "You could warn a gal next time. I thought you were supposed to be my Sensei."

I wrap an arm around the pole. "Hey, you got it right this time!" I offer her a high five. She doesn't accept.

She scowls. "Did you say something about timeouts earlier?"

The smirk on my face disappears. "Uh, maybe? It's just a game I like to play."

"Hm. Okay," she says, peering around the innards of the train.

Our car is nearly full with only a few standing-room-only spaces available. The underground train glides forward on the tracks, tilting slightly around corners and picking up speed on the straightaways.

I chance a look at Bryn again. "Is that enjoyment I see written on your face?"

She swats my arm. "No, it's fear."

I can tell she's lying. Her top lip begins to curl and she shifts from one foot to the other. This is the equivalent of a Disneyland ride but at the airport and for adults. There's no way she isn't having fun.

"You smile when you're afraid?" I ask innocently.

She glares up at me. "Doesn't everyone?"

"Only when we're trying to hide how we really feel."

Her lips part at my reply but the train begins to slow, making another stop to pick up more needy travelers. I keep my eyes glued to hers even as the doors peel apart and a throng of people enter and exit. Normally, I'd shrink under a gaze as intense as Bryn's. But I don't. Not here and not when I see parts of her soul that I want to know more about.

She breaks our eye contact, watching the train fill up even more. We're forced back closer to the opposite side to make more room. I press my palm on the ceiling above my head as the bodies filter in. But they don't stop. They keep coming, pushing forward and creating space where there isn't any.

Facing the door, Bryn backs up until she bumps into my foot. The recorded voice blares across the intercom and begins the inevitable countdown. More people appear out of nowhere, dipping and diving until they get a prized spot in a crammed train.

I don't have to look down at Bryn to know she's smashed up against my chest now. All of her soft curves are pressing into my hard lines like a dot-to-dot book. I'm acutely aware of the prickling sensation using my spine as a rollercoaster ride.

The smell of apples overruns my senses and before I can think better of it, I'm leaning in and sniffing the top of her head.

"Did you just smell me?" she asks. Or rather demands.

I straighten. "Huh?"

An elbow punches into my stomach and I grunt.

"What? You smell good."

It's more than how she smells though. This feels like I'm somehow able to breathe underwater. That isn't possible. But with her, I don't know. Maybe it is.

CHAPTER EIGHT

Rex

This isn't my gate. It's not my plane, either.

I'm going through the motions of a person who knows what they're doing. I've second-guessed myself at least a dozen times between the bar and gate N9. There's still so much I need to know about her. Bryn's womanly wiles have me taking risks I wasn't prepared to take before I turned around in the security line. I wasn't planning to go to Florida, but now I'm desperately trying to convince the gate agent that I need to. I have to. It's critical.

Half of my body bows over the counter, trying to catch a glimpse of whatever is on that top secret screen of hers. "Please. I need to get on this plane."

"Sir, your ticket had you going to California. There's only so much I can do here, and the flight to Florida is full."

Of course it is. Seattleites schedule their vacations during the rainy season, flocking to anywhere above seventy degrees so they can continue to wear their socks and sandals. I don't know how my mom deals with Gloom City nearly all year round. *Summer*, she tells me in her best Yoda voice.

I shake my head, peering down at her name tag. "Evelyn, is it?" She nods and so do I. "Don't look yet, but there is a woman sitting in the seats behind me, the one in the black panther outfit with her hair in that power-pony. Her green eyes that make you forget what day it is, and skin so smooth that she likely moisturizes every morning and night. And her voice…" my words drift as I give a low whistle. "Her voice might as well be a thousand angels humming softly in perfect unison; it somehow cradles me every time she speaks." I push off the counter and pretend to rock a small infant in my arms. Too much? Nah.

Evelyn starts to tilt to the side, looking to see if Bryn exists or if I'm making her up. I'm not. I wish I were. Not only is she stunning but every new thing I discover about her, I like. She's so different from me and apparently I want more of that in my life. One of me is enough.

Standing upright, Evelyn lowers her lids, assessing my intentions. My eyes plead with her. At least, I hope that's what my eyes say, instead of looking constipated or worse—creepy.

Her hands hover over the keyboard, and we're both waiting. I'm waiting for her to print me off a new boarding pass, and she's waiting to see if I'm full of it. Evelyn doesn't say anything but she does start typing away on her keyboard of possibilities without breaking eye contact. I stare back, amazed at how many words she's able to type per minute. She could break records.

The whir of the printer kicks up, and she slides a ticket across the counter, eye contact still going strong. I bite back a smile, which is nothing compared to what I actually want to do. I'm close to a full spontaneous touchdown dance. But I hold it in, if only to not embarrass Bryn.

Evelyn points a finger at me. "You better not waste this opportunity with her."

I cross my heart and hope to die, using my finger to pretend-poke a needle in my eye, something I haven't done since grade school. "I won't. I swear. Thank you!"

Her expression softens as I slide my new ticket into my back pocket.

She nods and turns her attention back to her computer, ready to pound those keys into oblivion. I do a slow turn and make my way back to Bryn.

She's hurriedly clicking through her phone then shoving it into her purse. Looking down at the book in her lap, she starts reading the very same one she promised to read for the duration of our wait. But I have other ideas.

"Good book?" I ask her.

"The best."

Her follow up yawn isn't as convincing. "Did you get everything squared away?"

I hook a thumb toward the counter and the blessed woman behind it. "Oh, yeah. All good, just checking that the plane is on time." Without waiting for her to ask more questions I don't have answers to, I continue. "Want to go on a walk and explore?"

"No." She continues to read. It almost looks real. "I don't want to carry my bags around."

"Evelyn might be able to help with that."

She swings her gaze to meet mine, but only briefly before staring back down at the most interesting words ever written. "You're on a first name basis with the gate agent?"

I sit across from her. "Yes, Evelyn is a doll."

"Good for you two," Bryn says. I wish she'd look up again. Those eyes. Those lips. Those cheeks that flush too easily.

I lick my bottom lip. "Alright, so no walking."

If I hadn't already noticed the slight twitch in her upper lip and roaming eyes on my body, I might believe in this crispy exterior she's leading with. Good thing I don't. She's a complete one-eighty from everyone I've been with. I've dated but mostly steered clear after Claire, my last long-term girlfriend. It's not like I haven't been attracted to anyone since her, but never enough to do anything about it.

Bryn is changing my mind.

I clear my throat and lean back. "What's your story?"

Exhaling loudly, she makes a show of digging around her purse and pulling out a receipt. Flattening it between her palms she slips it reverently between the pages, closes the book, and crosses her legs. "What do you mean?"

"Back in line, you said you don't vacation much. Why is that?"

She shakes her head. "I work a lot."

"So your boss doesn't believe in taking time off? What do you do?"

"I'm an architect. Well, I'm an assistant architect, which basically means I do a lot of the grunt work, spending hours in and out of the office working on projects and ignoring basic human needs."

I widen my eyes. "Sounds…"

"Like I'm sacrificing myself on the altar of deadlines? Yeah, I know."

I laugh. "I was going to say hard but gratifying."

"It was, at one time. Now I just find myself… stuck." She stares past me, her mind miles away. Shaking her head, she leans on the armrest. "What do you do?"

"Surf instructor."

She scoffs and says something to herself that sounds like, *guessed that right.*

"What gave it away?" I ask with an amused grin.

She peers over at me, the flush creeping into her cheeks before she even opens her mouth. "I, well, uh…it was the…" Her hand draws circles in the air around my person. "The hair, the…" When her eyes sweep over me in a way I'm starting to enjoy, I decide to jump in and save her.

"I can't seem to part with the long hair." I lift my hat and sweep a hand through my hair, gripping the ends in a firm tug.

"The tan," she blurts out. "You're very tan."

I chuckle, enjoying *perfect* Bryn tripping over her words. "Kinda hard to avoid the sun when I'm outside all day."

"Clearly." She uncrosses and crosses her legs. "Do you even use sunscreen?"

"No."

She crosses her arms now and tips her head to the side. "Coconut oil? Anything?"

"Nope." Though, thanks to her, now all I can think about is her rubbing coconut oil all over me.

I watch her throat move as she swallows. "I–I need to go to the bathroom." She stands quickly, grabs her purse, and points in the opposite direction of the bathrooms, a rosy bloom on full display on her delicate skin.

When she walks in the direction she pointed, then turns and walks the opposite way, I smile. Pulling out my ticket to Florida from my back pocket.

How many times can I make her blush on the flight?

Challenge accepted.

CHAPTER NINE

Bryn

Going in the correct direction this time, I shuffle toward the women's restroom, pumping my arms as I go until I'm safely inside the small sanctuary built in every public space. I didn't think he saw me take a picture of his backside and shoot it via text to Anna, but he did seem extra smug. How annoying.

The lighting in the bathroom feels darker, the tiles worn, and there's not another human to speak of, but I bypass all of those things and shove my way into an open stall.

Wrestling the button on my romper—yes, romper, because this is my day one outfit and not fit for airport attire—I finally get it undone and slide it down my body. As I finish, I hear a faucet turn on and someone clears their throat. But it sounds raspy and hoarse.

Was that…?

A deep, very man voice answers his phone, talking and laughing like he has a right to. I almost yell through the small slit in the stall that he's in the wrong place when I pause. Wait. Staring to my left then my right, I don't see it. Where is the mini trash can attached to the wall that's in every women's bathroom? Where did it go? I saw it, didn't I? It was just here. Sweat beads on my upper lip.

It's not here.

I look down and let out a silent curse. Rompers are comfortable. So comfortable that you forget how inconvenient they can be when you have to pee. Jeremy hated rompers because they took too long to take off, which is exactly why I bought it. Consider this my chastity belt.

Aside from sticking it to Jeremy, I'd even go as far as to say rompers seem practical when holding them up and admiring them on a hanger. You can bend without your shirt riding up or your thong hanging out. They're easy, breezy, *simple* when looking at them under the lights of the overly priced boutique store.

But not here.

Oh no. Not here in a men's bathroom you accidentally walked into, seated upon a toilet where your one piece romper leaves you more exposed than in the middle of a strip tease. I have nothing but my bra keeping me covered, though it does little in terms of warmth.

I hold my breath. If I breathe, someone will know I'm here, in this stall clutching my chest like a coconut bra. But I don't have coconuts now do I? I have two hands.

The strong male voice fades only for another to ring out.

"Bryn?"

My name sounds like it was spoken through a bullhorn and displayed on the Jumbotron screen at pretty much any sports thing. It would read: BRYN IS IN THE MEN'S BATHROOM. I jump, flailing my hands in front of all of my bare skin. There's too much of it. I hunch forward, using a small corner of the romper to hide myself. But it covers nothing and does little to stop the goosebumps from rising across my skin thanks to the arctic experience that is the men's bathroom.

I'm wishing for my day three outfit of shorts and a tank top or the maxi dress for day four, *anything* but day one's romper I'm currently sporting.

"Bryn?"

Rex. Exactly the person I don't want to see right now. I debate keeping silent but remember that he could've seen me walk in here. I'm screwed. "Uh, yeah, hi," I say sheepishly.

I hear a throat clear. "I think…"

"Mhm," I reply. I'm not going to admit the obvious—that I'm naked in a bathroom tiled with testosterone.

"I think you're in the wrong bathroom."

His voice sounds closer and I panic. "Don't come closer!"

"Why? Are you okay?"

"Fine. Totally fine." *Just naked*.

"Are you sure? Your voice sounds pretty high-pitched and…squeaky."

I close my eyes tightly. It doesn't matter that there's a door. Not when the half-inch gap on either side is now the height and width of a full size window knowing Rex is on the other side. "Could you just turn around?"

"Turn around?"

"Um, yes, please. There's a problem I need to fix." I stumble over the words to explain the hellish situation I'm in.

"Do you want me to help?"

"NO!" I scream, placing a flat palm in front of me to ward off his incessant helpfulness. He's so freaking kind, it's making me mad. "I can do it myself. It's just uh…" I stare down at my romper that has betrayed me in more ways than one today. "It's my day one outfit. I'm wearing a romper."

I hope this is all I'll have to explain and Rex will get the idea.

He doesn't. "Did you spill something on it? Do you want me to bring you any clothes?"

God, I don't think this moment could get any more twisted. Having Rex scour through my underwear, bras, and the full apothecary in my bag sounds like a nightmare. How am I supposed to explain the three different mushroom powders and loose leaf tea sampler I brought? "No, please don't. It's my romper. I had to take it off to go to the bathroom." Every single word has at least a five second pause in between.

"Ah," is all he says. "I'm turning around."

"Did you just leave my suitcase out there?"

"No, I left it with Evelyn," he says.

I sigh. The last thing I need are all of my essential oils stolen.

Standing, I hike up my romper and proceed to fumble with the button loop in the back. If being fully exposed in the men's bathroom wasn't enough, my outfit had to double down and make sure this would be the most awkward moment of my life. It wouldn't be a big deal if this one button weren't solely responsible for keeping the rest of my outfit from falling off. The deep slit in the back looked cute in the dressing room when I decided to buy it, not when my hands are shaking as I attempt to thread the loop around the world's smallest button. I am zero help to myself.

Dropping my hands to my side, I huff. "Rex?"

"Yeah?" he replies, voice low.

"I need your help."

A pause. "Uh, what kind of help?"

"It's my button. I can't loop it."

A longer pause. "No one else is here if you want to come out."

I'd rather not get caught in the men's room with Rex buttoning up my outfit. We'd be in a whole new category of awkward.

"Can you come in here? I don't want to come out there, you know, in case."

I hear his flip flops smack along the tile as his shadow becomes visible on the ground when he reaches my stall. He knocks once and I unlatch the lock, letting the door swing open wide enough for him to fit. He manages to squeeze through the six inches I allot him and I lock the stall.

I'm gripping the back of my romper at the neck to keep it from falling when we make eye contact. His hands hang long by his sides and there's something intimate about what I'm asking and what he's about to do. Mentally, I knew the space would be small for both of us. Physically, my body is hyper aware of how close he is. Emotionally, I want to laugh while burning this romper and hysterically cry at my embarrassment. Spiritually, I'm praying I can make it out of here without touching Rex more than necessary.

He twirls his finger indicating that I should spin around so we can get this over with. I do. But his smell is making it hard to focus. Saltwater and fresh linen. No, no. Maybe it's lavender. Whatever it is, it smells amazing and with little space between us, I'm inhaling him with every breath I take.

I pull my ponytail to the side but he still hasn't moved. "It's just the button at the top–"

"I see it," he says before I've finished speaking.

"Okay."

A light brush of his calloused fingertips grazes the skin near my neck and my breath hitches. Don't think I didn't hear the abrupt intake of his breath, too. His hands stop moving but if they stay hovering on my neck like they are, I'm going to go crazy. It's too much. These tight quarters, a delicious smelling hunk of a man, and so much pent-up need growling at me.

My chastity belt is literally broken.

He's trying to hook the loop around the button, but it's tiny. Even I struggled to latch it and my hands are a lot smaller than Rex's large man hands.

Damn it, stop thinking about his hands!

"It's so small. So tight, I can barely get it in there," he grunts.

A door slams shut, echoing in the small space and we both freeze.

Is someone…no, they can't be. Rex checked, right?

"Get a room," a voice yells before turning on the water and muffling our attempts not to laugh.

The poor man must have thought…well, we are…but not like that.

Rex's hands are still holding my romper up as he rests his forehead on my shoulder and lets out a hearty laugh. I'm joining him, equal parts mortified and on fire.

He must notice, too, because as his laughter dies, the already charged moment shifts. Now, it's heavy. Thick with attraction. I can't hide from him in here. Not with my clothes hanging off me in the tightest possible quarters with our skin touching.

Lifting his head, his breath is hot on my neck and tingles raise every hair on my body. It has nothing to do with how cold it is in here and everything to do with the inferno raging through my veins. I place one hand on the stall wall in front of me, no longer able to take it and needing the support it'll give when he's this close.

"Are you okay?" His voice is low and gravelly like he feels it, too.

I nod, words getting stuck in my mind while my tongue dries up. His fingers are moving again, attempting what feels like the impossible now. I stare forward, my hand still holding me up. That's when I see it. A hand-drawn, anatomically correct, penis. It's scrawled in black sharpie on the stall right next to my hand. *Real mature*. Who knows how long it's been here, but it's never coming off, that's for damn sure. And now it's staring at me, winking even.

"I think…I've almost…got it!" His hands retract and I can think again, breathe even.

I let out a whoosh of air. I'm so relieved. Between Rex's touch and the hand-drawn penis, I don't think I could've lasted another second with mostly clean thoughts running through my mind. "Great. Thank you," I reply shyly.

Needing to escape quickly, I go to unlatch the stall and he grabs my hand, gently pulling it back and away from the only exit.

"Wait," he says.

I peer over my shoulder and up into his steely gray eyes beneath his dark lashes. He studies me, eyes roaming around my face as if he's searching for his own lost words.

He releases my hand. "I should check to make sure it's still clear out there."

I blink rapidly, catching back up to speed with what's really going on. "Right. Yeah, of course. Good thinking."

Damn sharpie penis.

I smile and my insides cook like an egg on hot cement. It's a phenomenon how many times I've smiled at him today, despite my attempts not to. I don't know what to do with all this smiling. All of the newness of touching someone again is foreign. We don't have three point five dates behind us, friendship, or even basic information like birthdays or dental history. Yet touching Rex feels like something out of a book. The underlying sizzle is magnetic, mind scattering, and intense. I blame Anna for all of it.

He has to get out but I'm blocking him. Switching places becomes challenging when there's no way to do it without grazing each other. Do I give him my ass or my tits? Front or back? There's really no way to avoid some kind of full body brush.

I choose to face him—he's been staring at my backside enough—and realize at the last second he's facing me, too. We shuffle our feet to opposite sides and I try to suck in but that's only pushing my chest further into his. "Sorry."

"Don't be."

I don't know how it happens. One minute I'm grazing his chest with my own and the next our eyes connect and then our lips. Okay, I guess I do know how it happens.

His lips move slowly against mine. Heat, friction, and nothing else; a match being swiped against a rough surface. He cups my cheeks with his hands while I dig my nails into his waist. I don't know where this comes from—the hunger and desire as it pulsates through me. He angles his head, deepening our kiss, and I snap like that woman at the bar.

I drop my hands from his waist and sever our lips. "Stranger," I say through panting breaths if only to remind myself that I don't know this guy. He's sexy as hell, and the fact I just kissed him in a bathroom—a *men's* bathroom—speaks volumes to the egg scramble going on inside me, but I have spent exactly three hours with him. How can you really know someone in that short amount of time? He could have just gotten out of a relationship. Maybe he has a kid or an outrageously large Furby collection. These seem like important questions to know before kissing behind closed doors.

He nods like he understands. "I'm sorry. I shouldn't have done that."

"Don't be. I–I shouldn't have...we should just forget that happened."

He shoves his hands in his front pockets like he's trying to play nice and stay on his side of the stall that doesn't really exist.

I open and close my mouth so many times. I don't know how to ask these deeply personal questions. Do I want to know? Is it worth knowing? What would it change?

"I'm gonna…I'll leave." He unlocks the door behind him and slides out.

It's quiet again and I'm left alone with my own thoughts, forced to admit what's really going on here: that I have a crush on someone I just met.

CHAPTER TEN

Rex

Our short but loaded time in the bathroom stall continues to replay in my mind as if it's the only thing I'm capable of thinking about. And it's true. I can't stop.

My hands shook like a newborn foal learning to stand. They were clumsy and stiff as I attempted to shove the button through the loop. I can't even say that without getting other ideas. Who am I? When did I become the guy to kiss a girl in the bathroom stall? An hour ago, apparently.

Bryn is everything I didn't think I wanted. She's smart, hard-working from what I can tell, detailed, organized, funny when she isn't trying to be, sexy as hell. And now that I know she's wearing a black lacy bra under that one-piece contraption, I'm done. It's over.

She's reading again in the terminal sitting area and this time she pulled out her glasses. *Glasses.* As if she couldn't be cuter, now we're adding glasses to the mix, and I can't stop stealing glances as I sit across from her. She's adorable and has that hot architect vibe that makes me want to shove things off a desk and kiss her on one—hard.

I scrub both hands over my face. Thank God she can't hear my thoughts right now. It would freak her out. Hell, it freaks me out. Claire had been a friend of a friend that I had hung out with for close to a year before asking her out. And by saying, "I asked her out," I actually mean she asked me out.

I don't do stuff like this.

My dad told me he loved my Mom the moment he saw her. *When you know, you know*, he always said. It kills me that I can't pick up the phone and call him. Sometimes I forget and still try. He wouldn't have known how to answer his phone (he didn't get along with technology), but he would've had my mom's help with that.

"So, what's your story?" Bryn asks, staring me down through her glasses. The piercing look she gives me makes me sweat.

"What part?" I reply, hoping she'll start somewhere easy.

"You said you teach surf lessons. Why?"

I laugh. *Why?* "Because I love surfing."

She crosses her legs. "Yeah, but, did you want to be anything else? A doctor? Businessman? Did you go to school?"

Her questions make me feel like this is an interview. "I did go to school. I have my Master's in business, actually, and owning a surf school has been deeply rewarding. I'm my own boss. A regular nine to five isn't my kind of gig."

She nods slowly, crossing her arms and staring somewhere over my shoulder. "Have you…do you…are you seeing anyone?" she asks clumsily.

Evelyn's voice interjects over the loudspeaker before I can reply. "We will begin boarding shortly. Please have your boarding pass ready. When you hear your group, please come forward. Thank you."

I lean forward and shake my head. "I'm not seeing anyone."

"Have you…ever?" Her voice is hesitant when she asks.

"I've had a few girlfriends. Not in a while though." I rest my elbows on my knees. "It only takes one relationship to make you gun shy to try it again."

"You can say that again." Bryn's voice is quiet like she didn't want me to hear her, but I did.

"Spoken like someone who knows a thing or two about heartbreak. Was it recent?"

She pulls her glasses off and puts them away. "He was a cheating douchebag, and I'm just glad I realized it before it was too late. We were engaged." Her eyes remain on her lap, and I instantly have the urge to comfort her.

I interlace my fingers to keep from reaching out. I want to touch her. Run a thumb along her cheek and tell her I don't know the guy, but I'm one-thousand percent positive he's scum. I'd kiss the corner of her downturned mouth until it rose into one of her beautiful smiles.

"We are now going to begin boarding. Travelers with small children, military personnel, first class, or others who may need extra assistance, you may come forward," Evelyn says.

Bryn reaches in her purse. "What row are you in?"

Pulling my new ticket out of my back pocket I read, "Row twenty-four."

"Oh. I'm in row nine," she says. Did I hear disappointment in her tone?

It's at this moment I realize we are minutes away from being separated again. No, no, no. I didn't change my destination last minute to sit next to someone named Bearded Bob for the entire flight. Bob isn't Bryn. I didn't think about the fact we'd be on opposite ends of the plane. Conversation over. Stolen looks done for. I can't have this. Not now. Not ever.

"Rows seventeen to twenty-four may begin boarding."

She gathers her things to stand.

"I thought you were in row nine?" I ask, wondering why she's getting up when she's at the front of the plane and likely one of the last rows to board.

"Yeah, and I'll need to get in line soon. I like to be ready."

I stand, too, flinging my backpack onto one shoulder. "You could board with me," I offer. "Sensei approved."

She pins me with her stare like I just suggested we share some of her marijuana brownies. "That's against the rules."

"What rules?"

"The airline's rules. I'm not in your row. I can't get arrested twice in one day," she says definitively.

"I think arrested is a strong—"

"Rows nine through sixteen are now boarding." Evelyn interrupts again like it's her job.

I smirk. "Would you look at that. It's your turn." I follow Bryn to the long line.

Evelyn is making quick work of scanning tickets and repeating passenger's names back to them. Too quick. We're nearly at the front of the line, and I still have no ideas on how to prolong this time with Bryn. I can feel it slipping away. There are so many things I want to ask and now with a limited time to do so, I can't decide on where to start. Her family? That fiancé she mentioned? Her favorite color? Did she have braces? Is that why her teeth are so straight?

Bryn steps up and scans her boarding pass. "Bryn O'Riley, thanks for flying with us today," Evelyn says with a chipper tone. I don't miss the wink she gives me when it's my turn.

She takes my printed boarding pass to scan it. "Rexford Thompson," she reads, and Bryn stops and turns to face me at the top of the jet bridge.

"*Rexford?*" Bryn asks as if she's discovered a massive secret.

I guess she did. I never use my full name. I've always gone by Rex and for good reason. Grabbing my ticket from Evelyn, I wink at her and pat her shoulder as I approach Bryn.

I shrug my shoulders. "It's a family name."

She continues walking and throws a barb over her shoulder at me. "Alright, Sir Rexford."

I purse my lips. "At your service."

If only she knew how true this sentiment is.

We reach the end of the jet bridge, smiling at the flight attendants who are waiting inside the aircraft to greet us. The line stops moving, likely thanks to Bearded Bob who put his carry-on up above and forgot to grab his headphones. I'll take the extra few minutes. Thanks, Bob.

"By the way," I start to say, leaning closer so my lips are near her ear. "Your ex-fiancé is the one missing out. I'm sorry he couldn't see what he had."

Her back goes rigid as she stands taller, but she doesn't move her head. We are caught in our own moment where no one else exists. Not this plane, the other people, or the clock that continues counting down the minutes we have left together.

I don't pull away, too captivated by everything I've come to learn about the woman in front of me. If I like her this much and I only know a few random pieces about her, I can't imagine what the full picture will be like.

"Ma'am? You can go ahead now, the line is moving," one of the flight attendants says.

"Oh. Right," Bryn replies, lifting her suitcase over the lip of the plane and continuing forward.

The tension snaps with the reality of where we're at and what we're doing. I trail behind her, helpless to do anything else, and also, because I can't really go anywhere. I'm stuck on this plane headed to a destination I didn't plan on. But I didn't plan on meeting an incredible woman, either.

I widen my eyes as an idea strikes me. Ingenuity smacks me in the head like I do with the palm of my hand. I've got it.

I tap Bryn on the shoulder. "Are you sitting in the window, middle, or aisle?"

"Middle. Why?"

Perfect. "No reason."

Except, there is a reason.

CHAPTER ELEVEN

Bryn

I have one shot to make this work. Not to sound dramatic, but it's not like I can go around asking every passenger within eyeball sight of Bryn if they'll swap seats with me. I tell myself I'm going to ask one person. One.

Row nine comes into view and I see a man in the window seat, jabbering on his phone, and an elderly woman in the aisle seat, smiling at people passing by.

I see her before she sees me, which makes sense because this white-haired woman is not expecting me. Her hands are clasped neatly in her lap and her eyes are bright and cheerful. Exactly the kind of energy I'm looking for.

We approach row eight and Bryn shoves the handle of her suitcase down and begins to lift it into the overhead compartment.

"Here. Let me grab that." I shuffle around Bryn to reach hers.

She blocks me. "I got it. I haven't been lifting weights for no reason," she says with a slight laugh. Bending over she hoists the suitcase over her head, sliding it carefully beside the others.

I'm momentarily stunned. Not because I didn't believe she could lift her own bag. Because the definition in her arms have me silently thanking the weights she's been lifting. My mouth runs dry, and I try to recover before she sees my gaping mouth. Too late.

"Rex, you okay?" she asks like the kind human being she is.

"Yeah, yeah. All good." I lean in. "It's just Larry the Lawyer." I point toward the guy near the window having the loudest conversation compared to anyone else on the plane. Bryn looks as excited as a grounded teen.

"Just great. Well, I guess this is goodbye, for now," she says, her pretty mouth curving upward with some effort. "Maybe I'll come to the back for a visit."

I shake my head, fully aware of the line of people held up behind me. But the hope she just gave me, wrapped in a small package with a bow the size of Texas, is enough to do what I plan on doing.

Bryn slides past the elderly woman's knees and sits down. As she focuses on searching for either end of her seatbelt, I lean down and whisper into the elderly woman's ear.

"Excuse me, would you switch seats with me? I'm in row twenty-four, right near the bathrooms." I add this last bit like it's a selling point as good as a room with a balcony and a view.

Pulling back, I study the woman's expression. She seems to be considering my request, but I don't have time for consideration.

One shot, Rex.

I need to solidify this thing. Leaning in again, I lower my voice. "We're on our honeymoon." I tip my head toward Bryn. The words just slip out. It's as if my ideas are hoisted into the air and whichever one falls first is what I'm going with. Really? Fake marriage? We're going there?

"Oh, mercy," she clutches her chest. "Of course I'll move."

Bryn watches the exchange with curious eyes darting between the woman and me, but I avoid eye contact. I'm not proud of what I did—displacing this grandma—but it's done.

I help the woman gather her things and try not to feel guilty as we trade places. Resting a hand on her shoulder, I say, "Thank you so much."

Her smile might be wider than mine. "I'm so happy for you two—"

"Okay now, have a good flight!" I cut her off with three quick pats on her shoulder before Bryn can hear.

"How did you…what did she say?" Bryn trips over her competing questions as I sit in the aisle seat. Right next to her. I've won the honeymoon lottery if something like that even exists.

"She wanted to be closer to the bathrooms," I explain, kicking my backpack further under the seat in front of me and catching her biting back a smile. That hope rises up in me again, and I can't stamp it out. I don't want to. Maybe she isn't all spikes and points. The soft, sweet core is in there, too.

Bryn reaches into her purse for a pack of wipes and begins pulling one out to slather the armrests, tray table, and the entire back of the seat in front of her with disinfectant. I'm worried she'll try to wipe down the man's computer in the seat beside her or the balding man's head in front of me.

She catches me staring. "Here." Holding the pack of wipes toward me she adds, "They're natural. I swear. They only have essential oils in them."

As if this were the explanation I needed for the wipe bath she just gave every hard surface in her vicinity.

"Sure," I say, pulling out a fibrous cloth. I smell it, because now I'm curious. A minty, earthy smell tickles my nose and I hold back a sneeze.

Bryn snickers. "It's tea tree oil. Great for disinfecting. It's been documented in numerous medical studies for its strength in killing viruses and fungi. You can use it on wounds, too."

I stare blankly at my hand rubbing circles on the tray table. "Wow. All in this one little wipe."

"I read online how airplanes are a cesspool for bacteria," she explains with a shudder.

A smile tilts the corner of my mouth. I've never disinfected anything in my life, including my tray table that's apparently been crawling with germs that I can't see. I'm the kind of guy that drops food on the ground and still eats it. Once, I ate a chicken finger that someone else dropped.

I hold the virus-ridden wipe in the air between my thumb and pointer finger. "What do we do with it now?"

She reaches into her purse again and pulls out a small trash bag, peeling it open and shaking it, careful not to interrupt Larry the Lawyer beside her.

Holding it open for me, I drop my wipe in and she follows suit. Then, twisting the top of the trash bag, she rolls it up until it fits in the small pocket of the seat in front of her.

"You're really something," I say, trying harder not to stare at her lips than I did when I kissed them.

She stills and lowers her voice. "That's what my mother says, too."

I worry she may have misinterpreted my intentions. "I didn't mean that in a bad way. The opposite, in fact."

She smooths out the length of her ponytail and pulls it over her shoulder. "Thanks. I guess this is what happens when a perfectionist grows up with a hippie for a mother."

I laugh, not even trying to hide my amusement at her own description.

Her phone begins to vibrate and she pulls it out of her purse of tricks. "Speaking of my mother," she says, swiping to answer. "Hi, Mom…Yes, I'm on the plane…No, I haven't checked my texts…Yes, of course I brought chamomile tea to help me sleep… No, I didn't get to keep the brownies."

I chuckle to myself but when sitting this close to someone, it sounds a lot louder.

Bryn glances at me and then back to her lap, quieting her voice, but I can still hear her reply to her mom. "It was no one…Mom, you can't ask me that right now…What do I mean? I mean he's sitting right next to me…I'm not answering that question…You're worse than Anna. Okay, fine. Yes…I'll call you later. Love you, bye." She hangs up and scrolls through her phone. Tipping the screen away from me, she laughs heartily.

"Care to share?" I ask.

"Definitely not," she replies fast as lightning. "It's just my brownie loving sister again," she says, navigating to her settings to put her phone on airplane mode.

"Does your mom always call you at nine o'clock at night?" I ask.

She tucks her phone back into her bag, hugging it closer. "Yeah. I forgot to respond to her text, which usually warrants a call, or fifty, to make sure I'm not laying in a ditch somewhere."

"I can see where the serial killer/kidnapper inquisition comes from," I add with a laugh.

As the other passengers filter through the center aisle, finding their seats and settling in for the flight ahead, I can't help but sense Bryn's anxiety. Her fingers lace together as her thumbs chase each other at a speed that could set records. Their only competition are her legs that bounce up and down, shaking the seats in our row.

I tilt closer. "Are you doing alright?"

She whips her gaze to me and then away just as fast. "I'm good."

When the flight attendant's voice rings out over the speakers and Bryn jumps, I know she's lying.

CHAPTER TWELVE

Bryn

I'm not freaking out, you're freaking out. Okay, I'm totally freaking out.

Since when do planes take off like rocket ships? We are still ascending but this thing is seconds away from having to land in the ocean to prevent a crash. I know these things, because I binged every YouTube video on planes landing in large bodies of water. I bet everyone here will be wishing they listened more closely to the safety instructions. That's right, lady with your phone out, I saw you ignoring the flight attendants explanation of how to use the seat cushion as a flotation device. You were too busy checking out Brad on social media. Brad isn't here right now. You can't use Brad as a flotation device.

But it isn't just her. No one seems to be losing their marbles like I am. The other passengers sit calmly, hands in their laps, reading a book, or eating a snack. The other fool beside me has **HIS EYES CLOSED** like sleep is a viable option right now. We're about to die, but yes, please rest your eyelids.

Rex must be channeling a monk during meditation, because he hasn't moved an inch since we took off. I'm clinging to his arm with my fingernails, elbow, wrist, ankle, any part of my body that can get a grip. He's so unbothered that it bothers me.

"Is something wrong? Something has to be wrong. Why are you so calm?" My voice is strained and breathy like an animal panting in distress but I don't even try to hide it. We're crash landing before we even reach cruising altitude. The only two thoughts that flash across my mind are *I'm going to die* and Anna's text reply to the picture I sent: *Get it!* Both are wildly unhelpful.

"Just wait," he whispers in my ear, stroking my leg with his thumb and rubbing my hand that's coiled around his bicep with the other. The motion is familiar, as if he's been doing it for ages, but he hasn't, because he's a stranger. A stranger that I'm plastered to like a tattoo on skin that reads: *No Ragrats*. But I will absolutely regret this later. It's pitiful the way I'm pressed into him, the side of my boob attacking his arm in the most unholy embrace. He didn't ask for this and neither did his arm.

My breathing is rapid and irregular, indicating I'm about to have a heart attack. The flight attendant will be asking over the loudspeaker for any doctors or nurses on board to assist me. I'm a goner.

Why is there so much rattling? The sheer noise is deafening. I try to focus on the soothing rhythm Rex is rubbing into my leg. Back and forth with painstakingly slow motions. He doesn't have anywhere to be, nothing to freak out about, only a vast amount of time to sit and do exactly this. I like that about him. He's intentional and focused on whatever's clinging to his arm like a Koala bear. And right now, that's me.

I'm seconds away from calling my mom and sister to say goodbye. The "no cell phones in the air" rule is the only thing keeping me on the straight and narrow. The speed of the aircraft changes before I can do anything drastic though. The nose of the plane evens out and we're no longer cutting through the atmosphere trying to make it to space; we're coasting, riding on the waves of the sky: clouds.

At least, I assume there are clouds out there. It's dark and I had to forcibly close the window shade since it clearly didn't bother Larry the Lawyer that the city lights below became mere specs on the ground. I like the name Rex gave him. It's fitting considering he's dressed in full business regalia for a red eye flight.

"See. What did your Sensei tell you?" Rex speaks into my hair. "We're flying."

If he calls himself Sensei one more time, I'm going to karate kick him in the shins.

"Yup." I hadn't realized my head had found his shoulder at some point in the ride. Sitting up straighter, I place a hand over my stomach and breathe in and out. How can you accurately describe the brink of death?

"Fun, right? Landing is even better."

Fun isn't the word I'd use to describe take-off. I can't reply as I'm too busy figuring out how long it will take me to drive from Florida to Seattle. I'll ride horseback, take up running, or hide on the bumper of an Amish buggy if I have to. I don't care; I won't be doing that again.

I rub my forehead. "Landing?"

"What goes up must come down," he says, and I want to put him in a headlock.

I glare at him, hoping this mental image will be communicated by telepathy.

He drums his fingers on his legs. Message not received. "They'll bring a cart of drinks around soon. Try to relax."

Easy for you to say, Mr. Surf Instructor who looks like he wrestles sharks on a regular basis. I stare straight ahead. "Wine?" I ask. I'm still not past one word answers yet.

"You'll have to pay for it, but yeah, they've got wine," he replies.

Rex was right: no more than ten minutes later, the flight attendants wheel a narrow cart piled with cups and filled with drinks up the aisle. While waiting, I adjusted and readjusted my seatbelt, wiped my space again—once is never enough—and figured out what the button on my armrest was for. Rex told me, but I didn't believe him. I needed to see for myself that the seat could truly recline. It does.

Since we're in row nine, it doesn't take them long to take our orders. The woman, whose name tag reads Destiny, has bronze skin, dark hair, and a hearty smile as she hands me a bag of pretzels.

Lovely. Space food.

"Anything to drink?" she asks.

I clear my throat. "Yes, I'll have wine. All of it." I laugh a little too loudly. Destiny does not. "Um, he said you have wine?" I hook a thumb toward Rex. "And water," I add to clarify that I won't be guzzling all of their wine. "With ice, please."

Destiny nods, already reaching for a plastic cup to pour my water. She pulls out a mini bottle of wine and hands both to me.

"You're a lifesaver, thank you." I hand her my credit card.

Destiny gets a ginger-ale for Larry and an orange juice for Rex, because apparently he's five. The cart moves past us and I shake the wine bottle that's barely taller than my middle finger, unscrew the top, and chug.

"Wow. Slow down there. This isn't beer pong," Rex says quietly. His amused laugh doesn't go unnoticed by me. I feel it all the way to my toes. But maybe that's the wine? I need it to be the wine.

He smiles. "I bet you wish you had those marijuana brownies now, huh?"

I nearly choke on my next sip. "Shh. Keep it down," I scold, slapping his shoulder. If Rex doesn't quit, I'll be sending personal notes to everyone on this plane with the words: I DON'T SMOKE POT.

It's when I'm grabbing my water cup, the rim barely skimming my lips, that he decides to retaliate with a nudge to my arm. A waterfall of liquid spills down the front of me. It's deceiving really, the size of these cups. I underestimated the amount of water that could fit in one of them. Enough to completely soak my clothes as well as my bra and underwear beneath, apparently.

"Oh shit. Bryn, I'm so sorry!" He uses the cocktail napkin to mop up the water on my lap.

He isn't helping. The water was cold, made colder by the ice I just had to have, but as Rex dabs at my legs, hips, and stomach, my body is aflame. The light presses have now turned PG-13 in my mind and will be well on their way to R if I don't do something about it.

"I'm going to go to the bathroom and clean up. I'll be back," I say, rushing to clear off my tray table and grab my purse.

He stands and lets me into the aisle but the drink cart is blocking my way. I sidle up behind Destiny and tap her on the shoulder. "I need to use the bathroom."

She cranes her head over her shoulder. "Can it wait?"

I peer back to see Rex standing, casually chatting with a passenger sitting behind us and all I notice are his hands, his lips, his shoulders. Everything I've touched or grabbed. I can't go back there. Not yet. Not when his…and my…the water. "No, it can't wait."

Destiny nods and motions to the other flight attendant to pull while she pushes. I trail behind them, keeping my eyes locked on my destination. They angle the cart back, and I grab the handle for door number one. Locked. So I turn and come face to face with the red line indicating that door number two is in use, too.

"I might be here for a while, you go ahead," I tell Destiny who is already pulling the cart back. But not before Rex slips by. "What are you doing?" I ask in a loud whisper.

"Helping you." He points at his chest. "Sensei, remember?"

I cross my arms and coach myself through a few deep breaths. "I don't need help. I'm just getting cleaned up." I want his help, *all* of his help.

He opens his mouth to speak when he's interrupted.

"I'm Marjorie, by the way. And, Congratulations! How rude of me for not saying that earlier."

I knit my brows together as Rex's eyes widen.

It's the woman who was sitting next to me and is now in row twenty-four—Rex's old seat. I look up at Rex, unsaid words ratcheting between us like round three of a heated volleyball match. I want to ask him *why* we are being congratulated, but the way he tucks me into his side, the world's biggest clown smile painted on his face as he whispers quickly in my ear, *just go with it*, gives me some idea.

"Thank you, Marjorie! We're just so happy. Aren't we, *honey*?"

It's then that the pieces start to fit together.

CHAPTER THIRTEEN

Bryn

Bryn looks up and gives me a pinched smile. Okay, this is mostly good. She isn't frowning or stomping on my foot like I probably deserve for telling this dear old woman that we're on our honeymoon.

"Right, *honey*." She slinks her arm around my waist and settles it high on my hip.

Maybe this is better than mostly good. Maybe we're venturing into *amazing* territory.

She pinches my side and I bite down a squeal. Alright, I guess not.

"What will you two be doing on your honeymoon?" The woman asks, genuinely curious and invested in our story. The one we're lying to her about. She snickers. "I mean, besides the obvious."

Right. That's a comment I'm not ready to address. "Snorkeling—"

"–Whale watching." Bryn replies at the same time I do.

The woman's brows crease and she twists sideways in her seat.

"Both," I correct. "We're doing both. And other things, too. Like uh…"

"Swimming," Bryn chimes in. "And lots of shopping."

I tighten my hold on her shoulder. "Well, not too much shopping, *sweetheart*."

"Of course we'll be shopping, *peanut*!" Bryn exclaims loudly. "Now that we're married, what's yours is mine," she says, patting my chest with her other hand.

Damn, she's good at this.

I laugh nervously and capture her hand on my chest. "That's right…*sugar plum*."

Bryn's face flashes a look of disgust. "Can't wait, my big, hunky *T-Rex*."

"T-Rex?" The woman repeats.

Bryn turns back to the woman. "Oh yes, Rex here is shy about using his full name, the one written on his birth certificate. But I just *adore* it." She smiles and I glower. "Nothing to be embarrassed about, *sweet cheeks*."

She's beating me at my own game—the one I dragged her into—and killing it, in a good way. I bite the inside of my cheek and shake my head slowly, looking at Bryn through a squint.

"Take that one up with my mother." I slap my knee with a laugh. "Say, *boo*, you didn't tell Marjorie the most important thing we'll be doing on our trip."

Bryn's face pales as her eyes glide from Marjorie to me. "Oh, uh huh, that's right."

Marjorie laces her fingers together and holds them in front of her heart like this information will be the most delightful thing she's heard all day. I can't disagree.

I focus on Marjorie. "We'll be adopting three German Shepherds from a local shelter. It's like a souvenir but a million times better!" I squeeze Bryn's shoulder tighter. "My *sweet pickle* just adores dogs. She wouldn't let us come home without an animal so I said, 'Make it three!'"

Bryn squirms as my overly fake laugh leaps to new heights. "How could I forget, *fluffykins*!" She pats my chest a little bit harder. "And my T-Rex didn't know this, but since we're adopting so many dogs, the shelter is giving us a cat…for FREE! Surprise!"

Marjorie's eyes narrow and I think we may have just blown it, but she claps her hands and beams at us like we've just saved the planet. "A whole family! I just adore new love."

"It's new alright," I hear Bryn mumble beside me.

Marjorie begins telling us a story that I'm half listening to since Bryn is still cradled against me, her hip flush with mine. I don't even know if she realizes this is the longest we've ever held one another. But I do.

"I was married to my Henry for fifty-two years before he passed and you know what? Every decade felt like a rebirth of our love. It changes and deepens over time, but those first moments of falling were something else."

The sheen in the woman's eyes becomes more distinct. I stare down at Bryn, snuggled close and she's already looking up, gaze boring into mine. Her mouth falls open and my eyes drop to the swell of her bottom lip. Wet and plump like an apple. My mouth waters, because I know for a fact Bryn tastes better.

Marjorie points at us. "Like that! The love between you two is…" she begins fanning herself.

I swallow hard, peeling my eyes off of Bryn. My laugh is short, pulled taut with the tension I'm trying equally as hard to restrain.

One of the bathroom doors pushes open. Bryn drops her hands, politely excusing herself and heads for the bathroom.

"I think she likes you," Marjorie says.

I reluctantly peel my gaze from the shutting door with Bryn on the other side. "I sure hope so since we're married." I huff out a laugh.

"Mhm. I'm not blind, son. You know that, right?"

I'm not tracking. "What do you mean?"

"Your ring finger."

I lift my left hand, staring down at my empty ring finger.

"I figured you had to be pretty desperate to sit by her to ask an old woman to move seats." She crosses her arms and chuckles.

Scrubbing a hand over my face, I can't help but feel like a fool. "So you knew this whole time?"

"Of course I did. The lack of rings on both of your fingers gave it away, but I still stand by what I said." She nods her head emphatically. "New love is something special."

I shove my hands deep into my pockets. She said this already, but that was when Bryn and I were faking marriage. "We just met today."

She uncrosses her arms and slaps her knee. "Haven't you ever heard of love at first sight?"

"Yeah, in movies and books, but not real life."

She taps her pointer finger to her chin. "That's funny, because last I checked, we are in real life and the two of you are looking at each other like *that*. Are you saying it isn't possible?"

She has me there. I'm not saying it doesn't happen, but if it does, it isn't all that often. Love takes time and depth. I shrug as my only answer.

"We've got some work to do." She shakes her head. "See, my Henry and I were like the two of you when we first met. All heart-eyes and tingly touches. And there were *plenty* of touches."

I laugh with her while scooting forward to allow another passenger to pass, then take a wide stance to listen to Marjorie's life lesson.

"Those heart-eyes got smaller, sure, the touches not so tingly, but the safety, trust, and depth that come from a long-term committed relationship is what keeps that love growing."

I nod in agreement.

"So listen here, son." She inches her finger, beckoning me to scoot in closer so I do. "If love starts out as a seed and grows into a big ole tree, who's to say that seed isn't just as powerful? You can't have a tree without a seed."

Realization coats the edges of my mind, and I shake my head. "How are you so wise?"

She gives a hearty laugh at my response. "I learned to water that seed when I didn't want to. That's how."

I smile broadly, waiting for the appropriate amount of seconds to pass before I can go knock on Bryn's door.

"Go on ahead boy." Marjorie pats my arm and nods her head in the direction of the bathroom.

Standing up straight, I adjust my hat. I still can't fully comprehend all that my ears just heard, but my heart doesn't seem to have problems computing. I take two strides until I'm facing the door separating Bryn and I.

I exhale sharply. God, this is crazy. Bryn's going to call me a creep again and push me away. She's probably pissed about the whole fake marriage tangle. I'd be mad if I were in her shoes. Maybe she doesn't want anything to do with me and I'm reading into everything. Every graze and lingering touch. All of the conversations and tender admissions. The honesty and disregard for the pretense that comes with dating someone. She isn't pretending or putting on a front. She's real. It's not like I planned to see her and fall. I don't even know where I'm falling or how fast, but I am.

I don't know if I'm the only one feeling all of this but walking off this plane and wondering what could have been just isn't an option for me.

Just knock!

"Alright, alright. I'll knock," I say to my internal reprimands. Raising a hand, I rap twice. Nothing happens right away and I wonder if she heard me. I try again, knocking three times.

The latch slides to the right, going from red to green. Here we go.

Her eyes are wide when she sees me on the other side but then they soften. My blood runs hot, boiling beneath my skin when I see she's let her hair down. Dark strands cascade over her shoulders, the sheer length a total surprise since it's been caught up in a ponytail for the few hours I've known her. The hair, parted lips, and heavy breathing she's doing has the regular beat of my heart feeling like a complicated African drum solo beneath my chest.

I twist my hands together, fisting and unfisting them before dropping them to my side. I hadn't planned on what to say, though by the next words that escape from my mouth, I sure wish I had.

"I want to water your seed."

CHAPTER FOURTEEN

Bryn

I dab at my flushed face with a paper towel and lean my hands against the small sink ledge. I've already been in here for five too many minutes but I'm thankful for the locked door. I've been riding high on the fumes of being in Rex's vicinity. That's all it takes apparently. Close contact with a sexy surfer who is nothing like me.

The way Rex's hand held mine close to his chest, staring longingly into my eyes, did weird things to the beat of my heart. It's like the kiss we shared in the airport bathroom is all I could think about. He was lying though. It wasn't real. We had a fake marriage for a handful of minutes, and now I'm trying not to read into everything.

But I am. I absolutely am.

Why would he tell that sweet, old woman we were married just to sit by me? I exhale slowly, filling my cheeks with the excess air and pursing my lips. I'll stay in here for the rest of the flight. It's only four more hours. I'd have a bathroom and could ask Destiny to sneak me some snacks. Who am I kidding? I don't need snacks, just the wine.

Pulling out my ponytail with plans to redo it, I fluff it with my hands, letting it drape over my shoulders and down my back. I could moan at how good it feels to take out the elastic at the end of a long day. Maybe I did moan?

I finger-comb through my hair as the new plan I've titled "Ignore Rex and Drink Wine," forms in my mind. A couple of taps sound on the door and I startle. It must have been a mistake. But when a few more knocks hit the door, I widen my eyes in surprise. Undoing the latch, I fold the door to the side to see Rex standing on the other side. I imagined a disgruntled passenger looking to relieve themselves in the bathroom I'm hoarding, but it's far worse. I'm face to chest with him after being magnetized to his side, gripping the firm divots in his waist with my wanting hand, and nestling my hip as close as it could get. It made the accidental boob graze of yester-year seem like no big deal.

His hands are wringing together before he blurts out, "I want to water your seed."

I clutch the handle of the door tighter. "Excuse me?"

The lines on his forehead soften, mouth tipping downward as he shakes his head. Innocence is etched into every one of his features despite what just came out of his mouth. Is he insinuating…this has to be a joke.

His eyes grow wider and he stutters. "Shit. I didn't mean for that to sound so dirty, I–"

Grasping the front of his shirt, I pull him into the bathroom made for one that now holds two. He bumps into me and the wall during his journey. "You can't go around saying those things!" I fight the folding door until it cooperates and closes, finagling the sliding lock shut. Turning quickly, I stare up at Rex's hooded eyes and become all too aware of the now glaringly obvious mistake I've made: letting him into my personal territory again. I was hoping to keep him from spouting off more about my seed and watering it, but now that image is the only thing I can think about.

My back is pressed against our exit, our feet and my purse creating a sandwich pattern–his, mine, his, mine, purse–while the backs of his knees jam into the toilet seat behind him. "I, uh–I didn't realize how, um, small it was going to be," I manage to say with an unusually throaty tone. Beads of sweat break out on my forehead.

"Yeah, it's–" he clears his throat. "Tight. Even tighter than the last time we were in a bathroom together."

The laughter that wants to erupt out of me is a close second to the attraction I feel coursing through me. I bite my lip to keep it in check.

"At least it's a private bathroom this time." He laughs, the noise rumbling through his chest. A shadow of scruff chases the curves of his neck, causing my breath to snag.

I can't seem to look away. There's nowhere else to bounce my eyes when he takes up all of the extra space. The mood shifts once again as it does when each rise and fall of my chest causes my body to press closer to his. I'm not restraining laughter anymore. I'm suppressing desire as I consider his wolfish grin that tips one side of his mouth as he stares down at me. I imagine I could run my thumb over the dimple on that one side of his cheek and feel its shallow cavity. My fingers are itching to do so but I clench my fists, refusing to let them. It only takes one dimple graze and that will light a fuse that can't be put out.

His smile dims as his eyes linger, asking mine a question with the way one of his brows lifts higher than the other. I really have no clue what he's asking. I just know I'll say yes.

Raising his hands, he hesitantly and very lightly settles them on my hips as if he were trying to throw a rock into a pond and not create ripples. It's impossible though. His sharp inhale—or maybe that was mine—breaks through the loud fan noise that sounds more like a wind tunnel above us. The only thing louder is my pulse hammering away like Santa's elves on Christmas Eve.

There is still so little movement. If I couldn't feel his hot breath on my face, I'd question if he were alive. The scent of orange juice wafting between us is a mix of sweet and tang. I'm curious if it tastes as good as it smells.

His fingers stretch to their furthest reach, spanning the distance from the top of my hips to my low back. He licks his bottom lip and stares at mine. I finally compute the question he's been asking. Am I giving him the answer by allowing his hands on my hips? Do I want this? *Definitely yes.*

I've known Rex for milliseconds compared to Jeremy, but I've felt more in these few irregular heartbeats than the years I wasted on my ex. It's unnerving, really. Why is this the case? Jeremy had depth and substance to him. If he hadn't cheated on me, I'm sure we'd be married by now. God, I'm glad we're not. I want to dissect everything I'm feeling toward Rex. Compare and analyze until things become more clear. I consider reaching for the pen and notepad stashed in my purse at our feet to write a pros and cons list. I can think more clearly with a list.

STOP THIS RIGHT NOW!

I'm doing it again. That thing where I spin in circles over what was and what could have been when it comes to Jeremy. I'm done wasting anymore of my precious brain power on that tool. I want this.

Here, right now, with Rex. I'm craving orange juice all of a sudden. A craving so strong, it's visceral.

Placing my shaking hands on his forearms, I slide them up his biceps and trail along the sheer breadth of his shoulders. They're solid and structurally sound. *Pro.* I swallow the desire climbing higher in my throat and the longing swirling deep in my belly. I calculate the risk, waiting for the go-ahead from more than just my body. His fingers tighten at my waist, gently tugging me the last few centimeters until I'm smothered against him in the most delicious way.

"Is this okay?" he asks in a gravelly voice.

It only makes my skin prick with more awareness. I nod and blink rapidly, my mouth parting in hopeful expectation.

He leans down and I push up on my toes, dragging my body against the planes and mountains of his. *Pro.* Our mouths draw nearer, slower than slow. Achingly so. When his lips fold over mine, pressing lightly and then firmly, I match his fervor, needing to drink my fill of the sweet flavor that is Rex. We move in unison, the pace of our kiss becoming even more needy and frantic. Lips crush, skin burns, and my hands roam. I follow the trail from his shoulders, around the nape of his neck, and then into his hair, tipping off his hat and using my fingernails as the machete clearing a path. I pull and incite a groan from the back of his throat as his lips move over mine in hungry pursuit.

His fingers climb up my spine until one of his hands cups the back of my neck while the other falls back down, flattening against my lower back. He somehow twists me around until I'm pressed against the wall opposite the sink. The footprint we're occupying becomes even smaller and my purse tangles beneath our feet. It's reminiscent of our first kiss. The meld of our lips and eagerness of our hands. But it's different in that he feels like less of a stranger.

Breaking his lips from mine, breath scorching my cheek, he kisses his way down my neck inciting liquid fire to fill every one of my limbs. My knees weaken in response but he holds me up, paying special attention to the spot below my ear.

"Rex," I say, grasping for words.

He's too focused and grunts as his only response.

"Rex, tell me something about—" *oh, that feels good.* "Something about yourself," I finish. Yes, I realize what I'm asking and no, I can't take it back. He's less of a stranger than he was, but I need more. I want depth.

"What do you want to know?" He mumbles against the skin at the base of my neck.

Everything. I want to know about his mom that he said he was visiting, where he grew up, if he has any siblings, if he likes ketchup on his eggs. All of it. "Do you have any kids?"

"No."

"A Furby collection?"

"What's a Furby?" he asks into my shoulder.

"Never mind," I say, breathless. "Tell me something that not many people know about you."

He finds my lips again, pressing light pecks against them that linger long enough for me to forget I asked him a question.

Pulling back, he studies my face, desire in his eyes. "I'm allergic to apples." He dips his chin, intent on my bottom lip.

Pressing my palms against his shoulders, I push him back so I can see his face. "What? How?"

He shakes his head. "They make my lips swell up and my tongue feel funny after I eat them. So, I don't eat them." His smile morphs from playful to devilish, pressing his hips into mine and lowering his lips to where my ear and jawline meet. He leaves small kisses along the way until he reaches my mouth. *Pro*.

"Wait–*kiss*–hang on–*tongue*–" Grabbing his face, I pluck it from mine. "I like apples."

He shrugs. "I do, too. Just not real apples." Dipping his head he nuzzles his face between my neck and shoulder, dragging his nose along my tender skin and inhaling deeply. "I like how they smell."

I want to ask a multitude of questions like: What about homemade apple pie? Fresh pressed apple cider? Hard cider on a hot summer day?

Is this the first con?

Before I can add this to the cons list, he tangles his hands in my hair, running firm fingers along my scalp and pulling an unashamed loud moan from me.

My mind turns quiet, content to be caught up in a half-stranger's grip and relishing the feel of his body moving against my own. It's overwhelming to feel so much and intoxicating to know that it's possible.

Pro.

CHAPTER FIFTEEN

Rex

The small moan that escapes her mouth has me trying to get her to repeat it. I don't know how we got here. Together. Making out like teenagers. But here we are, locked in each other's arms by choice and by force, because this bathroom really is that small.

My hair falls across my closed eyes. She destroyed it with her fingernails, pulling and tugging my head into the position she wanted. Naturally, I had to reciprocate. Fingers intertwined in her thick hair, I can feel how smooth it is. I'm picking apples in an orchard, pressing them into fresh cider with nothing but my hands. I'll never be able to look at apples the same way again. It's potent and heady. Bryn is quenching my ravenous appetite. I don't need a Pink Lady or Granny Smith when I have her.

The way she tilts her head to the side and it lays loose in my hands as if it's too heavy to keep upright sends chills down my entire body.

I've done the same with her hips, moving them around with the rhythm of my own. Pushing them against one wall only to pivot and press her into the sink, our mouths staying connected the entire time. For all of the germ killing wipes Bryn used on her assigned seat, I'm surprised she hasn't whipped them out and bathed the restroom in her antibacterial oil of choice. She didn't even flinch when I braced the sink behind her and then touched her cheek with a wet hand. I couldn't let that one fly though. I immediately clarified it was only water from the sink. She didn't even care, grabbing a paper towel and handing it to me before pushing me against the opposite wall to devour my mouth.

She's a caged animal that's been let loose and all bets are off when it comes to what she'll do next. Tugging my bottom lip with her teeth, her hands trace the ridges and planes of my stomach. I'm a grateful recipient and a gleeful giver. That is until I start hearing the crashing of waves.

It's one of those moments I question if I'm really here, gripping Bryn's hip with one hand and the back of her neck with the other.

I trace her jaw with my nose. "Bryn?"

"Hm," she murmurs, clearly not caring as she presses against me.

"Do you hear that?"

The waves get louder and now I'm concerned. Where is that coming from? Why are we hearing waves? We are the furthest thing from the ocean, or we should be.

I stand straighter. "Are those waves? It's getting louder."

Her eyes wander as she listens. I see the moment that realization sparks. "My sound machine! In my purse."

"Your what?" I'm not sure why I sound surprised. At this point, I should be asking what she doesn't have in her purse rather than questioning what she does.

She starts to bend forward, one hand dangling to search for her purse at our feet while she uses my stomach to steady herself with the other. "Almost got it…Can you move back a little?"

"Um, no," I say with a clipped laugh. There is literally no space to move.

She stands upright again. "Alright, let me try this." Turning around so her back is facing me, she tries to crouch down but she's met with my unmovable body instead. "Ugh. This isn't working."

The crashing waves have reached full volume, the noise ricocheting off of one wall only to hit another.

A knock connects to the door. Our door. "Hello? Everything alright in there?"

Bryn widens her eyes and cups her mouth before whispering loud enough for my ears to hear above the soothing ocean sounds. "She found us! We're in so much trouble."

Sweet Bryn. She doesn't break the rules very often. Good thing I do. Raking my fingers through my hair to get it out of my eyes, I lean in and whisper back. "Just respond to her that you're fine. I'll sneak out when she leaves."

"Sneak out?" she bites back. "What if there's a line? A line so long it reaches first class?"

Another rapping on the door startles her. She nods, eyes still getting wider with every passing second. "All good," she replies. "It's just my uh–" She peers up at me, lowering her voice again. "What do I say?"

I smile broadly. "Tell her it's your sound machine. I'm sure she'll believe you."

Bryn crosses her arms and glares at me. Raising her voice again, she says, "It's just my sound machine. I need it for sleeping." She looks at me and shrugs.

"It's very loud. Can you turn it down? And you can't sleep in the bathroom," the flight attendant replies.

Bryn rubs at her forehead. "Okay. Got it."

Instead of bending over again, which I don't voice my disappointment for, she hooks the handle of her purse with her foot and lifts it up between us. It isn't done smoothly by any means, but she makes it happen. I look on as she rifles through her bag, bypassing granola bars, a label maker—say what?— and a cord for just about any device. When she finally finds the sound machine, her hands fumble with it, turning it louder before flipping the switch to off. Silence.

She looks up at me, shrugging dramatically. "What? I can't sleep without white noise."

"I wasn't even going to ask."

She sighs. "We should probably figure out how to get out of here."

"Are you sure?" I ask with a wink.

She flashes a saucy smile at me like it's nothing then bites her lip. "I've been discovered. If I stay in here any longer, Destiny will think I really did fall asleep and might plow the door down."

I place my hands back on her hips, shifting them slightly side to side. "That gives us maybe five or ten more minutes." My voice is hopeful, and desperate, but mostly hopeful. Now that I've tasted her, I know anything else I eat or drink will be flavorless.

Rising up on her toes, she slinks an arm around my neck, hovering her lips over mine as she speaks. "I can spare two and a half more minutes."

• • •

Bryn

IT'S BEEN TWO hours since Rex's hands were exploring parts of me only my loofah has seen for the last few months. A lingering burn of his hands on me are branded into my skin. Not even clickety clackety Larry beside me can ruin the memory of our bathroom moment. Although it's only gotten louder since he set up his portable office from the comfort of his tray table.

I peer over. His laptop is open and translating the words he is typing so furiously, you'd think he had a vendetta against the alphabet sprawled across the keys. He's wearing a pair of those tiny headphones, and I'm guessing he can't hear any of us considering the voice notes he keeps leaving himself. I now know way too much about the groceries he needs to buy—bananas, coffee, and gum—the doctor's appointment he needs to schedule regarding his athlete's foot, and some poor chump named Roger who had some colorful language sprinkled throughout his memo.

Rex leans closer to me. "Can you sleep with all of…this?" He nods his head in Larry's direction.

We don't actually know Larry's real name but that doesn't mean I don't feel like I personally know him at this point. He likes his air vent on full blast. Oh, and mine, too, since he basically commandeered it the second we sat down. He also likes late nights and appreciates a mediocre cup of coffee since he has consumed roughly four in the past hour. But I'm padding that amount and calling it six since I was indisposed for a while.

I adjust my neck pillow and lift one side of my sleeping eye mask. "No, I can't," I say quietly. "I want to murder his computer."

"That makes two of us," Rex says. "Do you want to watch a movie?"

I lift my mask fully. "It's two in the morning."

"So?"

I forgot I don't have work tomorrow. I'm preprogrammed to get twelve hours of sleep every night so I can be prepared to face all of the chaos my job offers. But I'm on vacation. No coffee runs or grunt work projects for me. "Fire her up," I tell Rex, gesturing at his tablet shoved in the seat back pocket.

He starts to set up his device, navigating to the in flight movie selection when a child's cry pierces through the silence. I jolt, sitting upright in my seat and looking around for the infant that needs assistance.

A little baby, who can't be more than six months old, continues her protests in her mother's ear as well as the small megaphone I'm convinced she's holding, since the noise resounds off of every surface. "Do you think she's okay?" I ask.

Rex looks at the child across the aisle from us with red cheeks and a wide mouth then turns back to me. "She'll probably settle down soon."

One Hour Later.

She has not settled down.

I have heard zero percent of this movie even with headphones on. "Do you think we should offer to help? Her mom looks…" I can't even say the words out loud. The young baby's mother looks somewhere between crazed and so exhausted she could sleep for the next twelve years. "I think we should help her."

Leaning in front of Rex, I wave at the mother who is two seconds from finding a parachute and peacing out. "Excuse me," I say at least five times before her gaze meets mine. "Hi, do you need help with—"

"Yes, here," the mother says, standing and passing her tiny infant across the person sitting next to her and the center aisle. But she can only reach so far.

Rex opens his arms, suddenly catching a tiny football dressed in a pink onesie. "Oh," is all he says, as the infant reaches an octave that I didn't know was humanly possible.

He looks at me as if I hold the answers to all of life's questions. I don't. I'm just good at guessing the answer to a tired mom's problems: help.

"Try bouncing her up and down," I instruct, shifting in my seat and miming the movement for Rex to copy.

He does his best. "I don't think she likes me."

What's not to like? I think to myself. "She's just tired."

I consider offering to take the little one when Rex unbuckles and stands. He adjusts the baby in his arms, cradling her upright against his chest, making shushing noises in her ear while rocking side to side.

The baby girl quiets, finally finding a position she can handle.

And Rex? His expression looks like he just conquered the world.

Me? I just want to conquer him.

CHAPTER SIXTEEN

Rex

Seeing Rex sway with the small babe in his arms is doing things to my insides that I can only chalk up to pure seduction.

He's a natural. A true, bonafide baby whisperer in jeans and a t-shirt. He disowned his hat a while ago and without hands to brush his hair out of his eyes, he's flinging his head to push it back like he's a model. Someone get this guy a box fan to really play up this sultry vibe he's rocking.

The way his muscles are in a perpetual state of flexing makes my mouth water. I touch my chin multiple times to make sure there isn't drool dripping down. Who knew he was packing all of that inside his six foot body of temptation. He's caught me staring no less than fifty-two times, and I'm still not sure what we're doing or what happens next. Other than the obvious, which includes making out and thinking about making out.

I'm saved by the baby's mother who finally returns from the restroom, looking ten shades more relaxed than before. Her hair is laying flat again, no longer arranged in chaos sticking up in every direction. The smile on her lips is wider than her lips can support, a marked change from the pinched grimace she had on earlier. Destiny must have hooked a sister up, or she is drunk on exhaustion.

She circles her arms in front of her chest, indicating Rex can give the child back now. He stares down at the baby girl, giving her a soft goodbye by whispering in her tiny ear.

STOP. But also, DO NOT STOP.

He places the baby in her mother's arms, smiling down and murmuring sweet nothings that I can't hear but can imagine.

All of a sudden, I need to use the bathroom. The urge is sudden and I bolt up from my seat after hastily unlatching my seatbelt. Facing him, I push Rex's large frame until we are careening down the center aisle toward the bathrooms. Together.

"Bryn, what are you—"

"Bathroom," is all I can say, hoping he'll decode my message. No time for meaningless explanations. So what if I'm pile driving him toward the back of this plane like I'm out of my ever-loving mind?

Both bathrooms are locked. What is it with people's bladders on planes becoming the size of a raisin? Not willing to wait, I push him into the cramped area beyond the bathrooms, pressing him into the cabinets and drawers that look like they were made for a space shuttle. I kiss his jawline in earnest. "Do you always hold babies like that?"

"Like…what?" he asks as his back folds over the hip-high counter, grabbing my waist on instinct.

I nip at his bottom lip. "Like, you know…*that*."

"I don't really hold random strangers' babies often," he says, laughing into my mouth. But I don't hear him complaining as he kisses me soundly.

"Ahem." A throat clears somewhere far off. It's distinct, but not, because we're in space, flying, soaring, and using each other's breath as our necessary oxygen to survive.

Arms trailing up my back, Rex cradles my face in his hands. Just as he rakes his fingers through my hair, ready to obliterate my freshly smoothed ponytail, the throat clearing gets louder. It's somewhere between a hacking cough and strained grunt.

There is no way that sound is coming from Rex. I can practically feel the low vibrations of his groan through his t-shirt and directly through his skin.

It's definitely not…*that*.

Rex uses his baby-cradling hands to pull my face away, breaking the suction of our mouths. It's then that I realize we aren't alone. Not even a little.

Destiny and her flight attendant friend stare us down like they didn't just enjoy the show we provided for free.

"Oh," is about all my brain can produce.

"Sorry," Rex adds. "We'll, uh…"

Destiny crosses her arms while the other woman lifts a forkful of what appears to be leftover lasagna into her mouth. They are both sitting in seats that fold out of the wall, waiting to see what we'll do next.

I have no clue.

"We're gonna…" Rex points in the general direction of our seats. "Sit."

"Good idea," Destiny says, hiding a smile.

Grabbing my hand, he tugs me back to our seats. We are no more than two steps into our journey that I feel the sudden need to apologize, "Sorry. For that."

He shoots a quick gaze over his shoulder. "Don't be."

Don't be as in the polite way of mostly accepting my apology or *Don't be* as in you want to do it again? "I don't really know what came over me. You were holding and rocking that baby and then…then…"

"Then…?" he repeats, stopping at our row and turning to face me.

The plane is quieter now. Everyone is tucked under their thin space blankets and most of the lights are off apart from a few. Rex's face is cast in shadows, and I note just how safe he makes me feel.

His stormy eyes lock with mine, and I look down at my fidgeting hands. "Then I needed too much all at once."

I'm not good at talking about what's going on in my head. There's always so much happening in there that when I try to pause and explain, things are vague and oversimplified. Does he get what I'm trying to say? What I'm feeling?

He reaches around my body, flattening his hand on my lower back and I gaze up at him. "If you ever need *anything*, I want to be the first to know."

Oh. Well, there's that.

I part my lips, still plump from dragging them across his scruffy throat, and nod. His words might just be more mysterious than my own, packing in so much information in one sentence that I'll have to decode its many potential meanings for the remaining two hours of the flight. I want to thank him for somehow understanding me but I still don't have the words yet.

Rex ushers me to slide in first. I sit and immediately buckle my seatbelt, wondering how I'm supposed to walk away unscathed. One-flight-stands aren't supposed to leave you feeling like you want more. More time. More kisses. More talks. Just *more*.

Rex sits as Lawyer Larry pauses his clacking to leave another voice memo. This one is oddly sentimental compared to the others.

"Hi, sweetheart. I wanted to be the first voice you heard when you woke up even if I'm not there. I miss you and love you so much." He clicks end on his message, propping his phone back into the phone holder suction cupped to the seat back in front of him.

The tears pricking the backs of my eyes surprise me. His message, that love…also, when did he install that phone holder? I want to pry like the nosey neighbor I really am and ask who his love is. How did they meet? How long have they been together? What's their story? Everyone in love has one.

And yet, everyone who has lost love has one, too. I lost Jeremy. Or more appropriately, he lost me. I've been trying to find myself again. To build up the parts of me that he tore down when he cheated. I thought this vacation would help me with that, but I'm realizing it's the people that are breathing life into my soul that are doing a far better job of reminding me that who I am is worth knowing. My sister, my mom, Rex, Marjorie, and somewhere in there, Lawyer Larry, too. I'm going to be okay.

Reaching forward to retrieve my purse, I dig around for the pack of tissues my mom always gives me. Last month, they had succulents on them. The month before that, there were five different dog breeds covering each one. I'll never go through all of the tissues she gives me, but she's religious about giving them and I'm devout when it comes to carrying them around.

I locate the package with my hand and pull. The rainbows smiling back at me only welcome the tears to fill my eyes more. I actually have a use for them this time but I can't work up the courage to break the seal and take one out. Love is overwhelming at times, knocking you off guard when you least expect it, like when you pull out a package of tissues that you carry every single day until you need to use one.

"Are you okay?" Rex asks.

I nod and offer him a rainbow tissue. He takes it hesitantly, holding it tightly in his hand.

There's something similar to the way I'm starting to feel about Rex. It's not long-standing and familiar like my mom's love but feels just as soft and welcoming as this tissue. I'm not damaged or fragile. I'm Bryn. And I feel more like her around Rex than I ever did with Jeremy.

The way my hair stands on end every time he leans close and whispers in my ear or asks me if I'm okay makes me want what Larry has.

I want Larry's kind of love.

CHAPTER SEVENTEEN

Rex

"Flight attendants, please prepare the cabin for arrival," the pilot chimes in through the intercom.

Six hours flew by, especially since the last two involved Bryn's head resting on my shoulder, arm woven through mine, and deep sleep overtaking us both. Even Movie Molly, enjoying her flick minus the headphones, didn't bother us.

I blink slowly, stretching my legs in front of me as far as the narrow space will allow, and do my best not to disturb Bryn. Neither of us have talked about what comes next, when the plane lands and we exit the bubble we've blown together. For now, I allow myself to soak in the comfort she's finding in my arm. Later will come.

Bryn startles, flailing her arms and legs suddenly. I stroke her arm. "It's okay."

She pushes the sleep mask off her face. "I thought we were going down."

"We are, but not in the way you think. We're about to land."

"Oh." She grabs her purse from the floor and hoists it onto her lap, tucking neck pillow, sleep mask, and yes, sound machine back inside. She exchanges it for something else. "Do you want some gum?"

I smile. "Sure." I grab a piece and unravel it from the wrapper, placing it on my tongue. The biting mint wakes up my senses as I begin to chew.

Bryn does the same, unwrapping, biting, chewing, but the movements seem more provocative when she does it. "I read online that it helps with the pressure when landing."

Of course she did. I've never met anyone with a more varied search history than this woman.

The plane begins its slow descent, shaving off ten-thousand feet at a time until the sound of the landing gear doors opening and wheels dropping alerts us of what's to come. "They are lowering the wheels. Almost there," I say, looking over at Bryn, chomping her gum vigorously. Reaching for her hand, I lace our fingers. We haven't done this yet, and I'm lacking an explanation for why it feels more erotic than having my tongue down her throat.

She stares at our joined hands and squeezes tightly. "Almost there," she repeats.

All I can do is stare into her bottomless green eyes and nod. I'm not the only one thinking that "almost there" means "almost over." This thing we've somehow managed to create with each other is special. It's not a relationship. It's not a date. It's definitely not just friendship. But it is something.

The whoosh of air being held back by the wing flaps fills my ears. Movies, cries, and all other sounds are hushed as we wait for confirmation that we've landed. The pilots expertly lower the wheels and then the nose of the plane to the runway, our speed decreasing until we're taxiing and the quiet becomes loud. People pull out their phones, calling loved ones to let them know they've arrived. Conversations between neighbors resume, and the flight attendants come over the intercom to confirm where we are and that the weather is arm-pit-stain hot at six in the morning.

I squeeze Bryn's hand, my gaze swinging to study her face. Her eyes are closed, her body rigid against the seat, but it's the placement of her other hand that has me laughing. She's gripping Larry's arm beside her, nails and all.

"Bryn? We've landed," I assure her, prying her hand away.

She exhales. "Sorry, Larry. I…this is my first flight."

Half moons line the inside of Larry's forearm, but he just smiles politely and nods like this is a common occurrence for him. Maybe it is. Then, Larry's brows crease. "Larry? My name is Steve."

Bryn stumbles over words that make no sense.

"Steve!" I repeat obnoxiously loud and reach to shake his hand.

He reciprocates, but reluctantly. He's got that lawyer scowl down pat. "So, uh, what do you do for a living?" I ask. I can't help myself. Steve has just become the most interesting person on this plane.

Steve smiles. "I'm a snorkeling guide."

If my mouth isn't hanging open, it should be. "Snorkeling?"

He nods enthusiastically.

I want to ask more clarifying questions like why he's wearing a button up and tie with a briefcase and loafers but Bryn finds her words.

"And your partner? Does she snorkel, too?" Bryn asks.

Steve raises one eyebrow and studies Bryn.

"I heard you leave her a message earlier," she adds in a rush.

"Ah, yes. My wife. She hates snorkeling." He laughs. "But she loves me."

I smile wide just as the plane comes to a stop and the seatbelt sign disappears.

Staring back at me, Bryn smiles with relief. "We're here. We made it."

Her use of the word *we* doesn't escape me. "We're here," I repeat, my voice coming out in a whisper. I can feel things changing already, and I'm desperate to keep us together for a little longer. I lean closer to her, smelling the mint on her breath, and press a chaste kiss to her lips. We've already crossed a few PDA boundaries on this trip, what's one more?

Her eyelashes fan across her cheeks and are slow to open, but when they do, I see exactly what I feel.

We're not ready to say goodbye.

WE STAND AROUND the baggage claim carousel, waiting for the luggage to drop. It's like waiting for a new album to hit the iTunes store but a lot less cool.

"What does your bag look like?" I ask Bryn. "I'll grab it."

"They're silver with pink tags tied to one of the handles," she explains. "Don't forget to bend your knees."

I make a show of bending my legs in a lunge position, stretching until my jeans are pulled taut over all of my angles. Bryn's breathy laugh is all I need to fuel me.

The carousel starts moving, indicating the luggage is on its way. We watch as different colored bags are propelled down a ramp, sliding against the edge and moving in a slow circle. People begin to press closer to the front, looking and waiting to grab their suitcases. I do the same, bracketing my hips with my hands in order to give an elbow's width of space on either side of me. I don't expect Slim Jim or Tiny Tina to put up a fight, but I'm ready just in case.

"There it is!" Bryn yells from behind me, pointing enthusiastically at her suitcase.

"Got it!" I squat lower, preparing to use my knees to brace the sheer size of this thing. It's moving at a snail's pace and giving me every opportunity to plan how I'll welcome her luggage into my arms. It's huge, nearly twice the size of Bryn's carry-on suitcase.

Slim Jim pulls his average size bag from the carousel first. A good show of focus and physical strength. I give him a solid eight.

I scan the luggage to assess where to grab and what will be the best distribution of weight. I turn and wink at Bryn. Why? Because I'm a male that likes to flex every once in a while. I know she's watching. So is Tiny Tina but I think for different reasons.

I bend lower, leaning until my fingers tighten around the handle. I'm pulling and tugging but the suitcase is heavy. I have to use my other hand to grip it and hoist it over the small lip before her luggage decides to take me on the circular joyride.

I've done it. Strength and determination have me proudly rolling Bryn's suitcase over to her.

"Thanks! Good job," she praises and I peer around at the other travelers that I envision are holding up signs with the number ten scrawled on it.

I smile. "Ready?"

"Not yet," she says, drawing out the words. "I have one more."

Of course she does. "No problem." I'm only sweating.

"It's a little bigger."

Of course it is. "I got it."

"Same color, same pink tag," she says to my back as I walk up to the whirligig.

It's bigger, I repeat to myself. It's fine. I'm fine. I got this, just like I assured Bryn. I'll use more legs this time. More abs, glutes, triceps, quads, calves. Basically every muscle group is going to need to pull their weight here to get this suitcase.

I exhale. Here it comes. Silver, pink tag, big. If the last bag was twice the size of her carry-on, this behemoth is twice the size as the last one. I gulp and slap my thighs like a sumo wrestler ready to destroy my opponent. But not actually destroy it. More like rescue it and bring it back safely to Bryn.

Gripping the handle with both of my hands from the start, I quickly realize I am no match for whatever Bryn decided to bring on this trip. Her entire apartment? Every essential oil that she owns? Bricks?

We're going to need to do the tuck and roll.

It's not pretty, but it has to be done. Shuffling my feet to keep up with its slow progress, I tuck my hands under one side and roll it off the conveyor belt like a beached whale. It does nothing to help me and I'm positive I'll be icing my Gluteus Maximus later. This suitcase has no business being here. No human has any business using it. How did Bryn carry this?

When it's finally upright, I hear what sounds like mechanical and plastic parts shifting inside her bag.

Tools. She brought tools on her vacation. Makes sense.

Rolling it over to Bryn, slightly out of breath, I ask, "What the hell is in here?"

"You should know by now I like to come prepared." She smiles. "It's my air purifier."

"Your what?"

She rolls her eyes as she scoots her bags closer together. "My air purifier. I'll be staying in a rental house and who knows what kind of paint, carpet, smoke, or mold will be in there? I'm not about to let that ruin my trip."

I nod slowly, trying to fit an *air purifier* into any of the possibilities I considered. Nope. There's no way. Again, this woman has taken what I thought and spun it in circles so many times, I'm dizzy. The only thing I can see clearly is her mouth, tipped into a smile that I see every time I close my eyes now.

"I should, uh…I'm going to call an Uber," she says.

Our smiles fade. "I'll help you with your bags."

"Thanks." She pulls out her phone. "Are you getting picked up?"

My mind goes blank. "Uh…I'll help you out first. Who else is going to drag your air purifier?" I respond with a smile.

She nods slowly, and starts navigating through the app. "What about your suitcase?"

"I only have a backpack."

She glances between me and her phone. "That checks out."

While she scrolls for eternity, I feel like I should ask her out, see where she's staying, but now that we're here, on the ground, with suitcase nesting dolls filled to the brim, I can't seem to find the words. I found the actions to follow her, buy a ticket, and make out with her. But now, reality sets in.

We don't live near each other. How could this work? We've never been on a date before. I've only kissed her. And, well, she kissed me. But what right does that give us to start something long distance? What if she isn't looking to date?

"Done." She puts her phone in her purse. "Jen will be at the pickup zone in five minutes."

"Great." I stare at her and shove my hands in my pockets.

"Awesome."

"Splendid."

"Wonderful."

"Excellent."

She clears her throat. "Okay, well, I'm out of adjectives. I should probably go to the pickup zone and wait."

The mood turns sour. "I'll help you." I swing my backpack onto my shoulders, grab the handle on the rolling bag containing the air purifier, and trail Bryn to the designated ride-share lot. I have five minutes to decide what to do next, and I'm kicking myself for not using the six hours it took to fly here to figure this out.

Exiting the sliding doors, we're met with a rush of warm, pre-dawn air with enough moisture to choke on. The sun is rising behind a few low hanging clouds, promising the day is here and the night has gone. I want to shove the sun where it doesn't shine, because those are the hours of the day I met Bryn. I want to take us back to the moment we met in the security line and experience every piece with her again.

But I can't.

We're stuck in the present and looking forward to an unknown future. I could ask if she needs a Sensei to teach her how to be a beach bum, invite myself, or simply beg her to spend all of her future hours with me that I'm greedy for.

Waiting for the driver, we silently watch vehicles filter in and out, picking up family, friends, lovers, and strangers, to escort them to planned adventures together. Our adventure wasn't planned though, and therefore, I don't have a stake in her itinerary.

Bryn looks down at her phone. "She'll be here in two minutes."

I shift to my other foot, tapping a rhythmic tune on the suitcase handle.

What are you going to do, Rex?

I stare at Bryn, taking in the tiny details that I can't ignore. The way the wind tousles her slightly more disheveled ponytail (thanks to me) and she fans herself to fend off the change in temperature. The way she squints against the bright lights of nature and closes her eyes, if only briefly, to inhale the fresh air. The way her lips are smooth and naked, reminding me exactly what they felt like against my own. Sliding, biting, pressing. A flood of sensation hits me.

Bryn's phone dings. "One minute. She should be pulling up soon." Her gaze swings to mine and now we're both staring. Do I ask? Should I let her go? Ask for her number for the next time I'm visiting my Mom? Bryn deserves everything. I want her to have all of the things she's never had. Does that include me?

Her eyes roam my face, landing on my lips. She inhales and I do, too. Our memories together, though only hours long, are there. Ingrained in my thoughts from now until forever. My lips part to say something to mark this moment in our shared history just as her Uber pulls up to the curb.

Bryn breaks our eye contact first when Jen hops out to say hello and help with her bags. I help, too, my body on autopilot. It's a group effort to lift the air purifier into the trunk, but we manage.

I nod at Jen, walking to the side of the vehicle to open Bryn's door. She pauses like she wants to say something, too, but doesn't have the words. The seconds tick by until Bryn rests her hand over mine, squeezing once and leaning forward to press a kiss to my cheek. I close my eyes and savor the feel of her lips on my skin one last time.

It ends far too soon and before my eyes are fully open, Bryn is already lowering herself into the car. The warmth of her mouth is ingrained in my skin and I consider what I've done to get here, with

Bryn. I can't make myself close the door despite Jen's urging.

It's then that my dad's words come barreling into my mind.

Some people come along that are worth risking for.

Marjorie's laugh cuts through the memory, adding her own.

You can't have a tree without a seed.

Slapping the roof of the car, I bend down and look into Bryn's wide eyes.

"Wait!"

CHAPTER EIGHTEEN

Bryn

My pulse is beating so fast I'm positive Jen is going to say something from the front seat. She doesn't, but neither does Rex. His eyes were still closed as I lowered myself into the car, unsaid words eating me up.

"Um, you have to shut the door. I've already been double-parked here for long enough," Jen says to Rex, but he looks like he's underwater and doesn't react to a single word.

I can't decipher the feelings squeezing at my heart. All of my good sense and life trajectory tells me to let this surfer be taken by the waves. But then I remember how he looks at me. Like I'm the only one in the room. It makes my stomach swirl. And the electric current we create when our lips are connected—we could provide clean energy to an entire city.

I set my purse beside me as Rex yells. "Wait!"

"Thank God," I say immediately, clutching my chest. I look back up into his eyes. "I can't take this."

"Me either," he adds. "Look, Bryn. I need to tell you something."

The swirls in my stomach begin to knot as I expect him to tell me he's a mermaid that was granted one wish to walk the land for a day. Hang on. No, that's not right.

"I'm not supposed to be in Florida," he says.

I shake my head and touch the base of my neck. "But you're in Florida."

"Yes, because I bought a ticket after we met. I should be in California. But I'm not."

"You're not."

"No, I'm not. I'm here. And you're here." He opens the door wider and slides into the seat next to me.

"I'm here," I say, trying to make sense of what he's telling me.

"I bought that ticket after we met, because I felt something with you. I know it sounds crazy and you'll probably call me a creepy stranger again, but I had to." His eyes plead for me to understand.

"How? W–Why?"

"My dad used to tell me that he fell in love with my mom the moment he met her and said that some people are worth all of our risk. I would always nod and agree, half-believing it could happen to me. But I think it did. When I turned around and saw you, my mouth went dry and my palms started sweating. My palms never sweat."

"Never?" I ask.

He shakes his head and reaches his hand across the center seat and brushes his thumb back and forth along my cheek. "After we started talking, I knew that you were worth that risk. So, I bought a last minute ticket to Florida to see if maybe you felt the same way and if my feelings would lessen. They didn't. And when we kissed, I felt *everything*."

"Everything," I repeat, unable to actually find any other words that aren't his.

"I really, really like you, Bryn," he admits.

I exhale and reach for his hand still stroking my cheek. "I like you, too." So much, I want to add. More than I should or what makes sense for someone like me and a man like him. We're opposites, polar ends of a magnet being drawn together by the sheer force of our hearts.

He relaxes into the seat like my admission is a weight off his shoulders. "I want to water this seed, and I don't care how dirty that sounds. I mean it in every way that you'll let me show you. I want to know every part of you, Bryn."

I nod, tears welling up in the corners of my eyes as I pull him close and kiss him like I never want to stop. He responds in earnest, scooting closer until our knees are knocking together and our noses dance, tipping and turning our heads to taste every angle of each other.

"Um, so, are you gonna ride with us then, or what?" Jen asks from the front seat.

We pull apart and Rex stares down at me, his breath mingling with mine. "What do you think?"

I bite my lower lip and nod. "I want our differences, the conversations we haven't had yet, and I want to water this seed with you." I press my forehead to his.

Jen stares us down through her rearview mirror. "Please don't do any of that in my car though."

We both laugh and confirm none of that will be happening here while Rex removes his backpack and buckles his seatbelt. I wait for the regret to show up, to slither into my thoughts and warn me that I'm making a big mistake. But they never come. Instead, when Rex laces his fingers with mine, I study the way our hands fit together. I've never been more okay to disown my plan than I am in this moment.

I may even wear my day three outfit on day two…

Nah, that would just be reckless.

EPILOGUE
One Year Later

Bryn

The sound of crashing waves on the beach wakes me. But they aren't at the beach. They're here, in our rented condo, next to the bed, and inside my sound machine.

I rub Rex's arm that's slung across my stomach, inhaling every one of his scents that are as familiar as my own. His leg drapes over mine and his bare chest presses up tight to my back, warming me from the inside out. This is how we've woken up nearly every single day since the first time we came to Florida, minus the few scattered weeks Rex traveled back to California to finish teaching his surf lessons and close up shop. That time was torture.

We compromised and moved to a small island outside of Seattle that's only accessible by ferry boat. It's a short boat ride to the city if we need, but our small bungalow on the Puget Sound is like a giant exhale each and every day. I don't need the city like I thought I did, so I quit. And though there aren't many waves for surfing in Washington, Rex told me with confidence, "I'll find something to do."

And he did. He started "Island Adventures," a place where locals and tourists can rent electric bikes, canoes, paddle boards, and more to explore the beauty of our home. I help him with the budget and accounting. Numbers and how they work in a proper order make sense to me. We're both doing what we love now. Together.

Rex's mom is thrilled to have us both close by. And after a few visits, my mom decided she needed a taste of island life in the middle of the Pacific Northwest. She owns a yoga studio in town and comes over for dinner often. Maybe a little too often.

"Rex," I say, squeezing his arm. "We should wake up."

"Hmm," he grunts.

"I have a whole plan for us today. Snorkeling, whale watching…shopping," I add.

He pinches my side, and I squeal. "No. More. Shopping," he mutters into my hair.

I flip around to face him, brushing his long hair out of his eyes. "Okay, fine. But we only have a week here, and I want to do everything we did the first time we came," I say resolutely.

We've been in Miami for five hours and if it were up to me, we would have started our day immediately after our red eye landed. I'm riding on the high of having been proposed to in the most spectacular way. It was halfway through our flight when the flight attendant, Freddy, said he needed to talk to Rex. I watched him trail Freddy to the front until I could no longer see him.

But then, I heard Rex over the intercom. His voice was loud and shaky as he proceeded to rap me a love song about how we met. I laughed and smiled the whole time until Rex was back by our seats, kneeling in front of me with an emerald engagement ring that he pulled out of my purse. I didn't even know it was in there!

Before any more words can pass between us, a seventy pound, four-legged creature leaps onto the bed and begins excitedly licking our faces and stepping all over us. "Griffey!" We both scream. "Get down, boy!"

Griffey doesn't get down, but he does wag his tail in Rex's face. "I can't believe you insisted on bringing him," he says, using his arm to shield his face.

Reaching up with both hands, I scratch behind Griffey's chocolate colored ears, squishing his face together and talking to him like the big baby he is. "We couldn't leave our whittle baby at home all by himself. He'd miss us too much. Wouldn't you, boy?"

Griffey barks in agreement as he sits on Rex's chest. "Can't. Breathe," Rex grunts, shifting Griffey so he isn't crushing his lungs. "And the fact airport security let you," he adds.

"He's an emotional support dog," I protest.

"And you couldn't have brought Jasper? He would've actually fit under the seat."

Shortly after Rex moved in, we both agreed that we needed to face our fears. We got our chocolate lab, Griffey, when he was six weeks old and brought home our shelter cat, Jasper, a few weeks later.

I laugh. "He would have clawed his way out until he could sit on your lap and you know it. He hates being anywhere else."

"Yeah, you're probably right." Rex pushes Griffey off of his chest, guiding him off of the bed before drawing me closer and nuzzling his face into my neck. "Let's stay here all day." He runs his thumb over my engagement ring.

"And miss out on swimming with dolphins? No way!" I playfully shove at his chest and he captures my hands, pulling me close and kissing me soundly.

"Ew, morning breath," I say while attempting to wiggle free.

Rex doubles down and tickles my sides. Griffey decides he needs in on this and jumps back on the bed, stomping his big lab paws all over us.

"Okay, okay, I surrender!" Rex says. "What's for breakfast?"

I pretend to throw a ball for Griffey and he takes the bait, leaping off of the bed and bolting out of the room to find the imaginary ball. I sit up quickly before he can come back and alert me that the ball has disappeared into thin air. "Your favorite," I tell Rex. "Oatmeal."

He smiles, half of his face still buried into the pillow. "Lies. I only like oatmeal cooked a certain way."

"I know." I slip on my robe and push my feet into my fuzzy house slippers I absolutely brought from home. "I brought the InstantPot."

He pushes up on his forearm. "You what?"

InstantPots are pretty damn amazing. Did you know you can thaw meat, make soup, rice, and shred chicken in a matter of minutes? Oh, and it makes the best oatmeal.

"Of course I brought it. It's my emotional support cooking device." I pad out of the room before I can see Rex shake his head. He'll change his mind when he takes his first bite.

. . .

Rex

I WANT TO be mad that she packed the InstantPot in the duffle bag that almost broke my back but those feelings wane with every bite of oatmeal. Bryn doubled down and also brought dried blueberries, hemp seeds, and raw honey from the bee farm on our island. Every bite tastes like home. Our home.

Bryn's phone rings on the kitchen table, and I grab it before she can. Swiping, I answer on her behalf. "Hello?"

"Rex. Why are you answering Bryn's phone? Oh no, is Bryn in trouble? Are you in the emergency room? What's wrong?"

"Hi, Anna."

"You're saying my name all weird. What's really going on?"

"I don't know. Maybe the fact that you're interrupting our vacation?" I offer.

"Oh. Right. Well, I need to know. Did you do it?"

I laugh and stare at Bryn who takes a seat beside me. "By *it* I can only assume you mean propose?"

"God, yes. I'd never ask you about the other kind of *it*. Bryn tells me that information."

"What? Really?" I sit up straighter and glare at Bryn. "What does she say?"

"Oh, never mind that! Did you propose?" she yells.

"I did." I smile at Bryn, because I can't seem to find any other reaction these days.

"What did she say?"

I pause. "Is that a trick question?"

Bryn snatches her cell phone and puts it on speaker. "Yes, Rex proposed. No, I haven't told Mom so don't you dare. And yes, I said YES!"

Screams of elation fill the small kitchen and dining space, forcing me to plug my ears. Griffey bolts up from his sleeping position on the ground and anxiously paces around Bryn's chair, barking and adding more noise to the mix.

Bryn animatedly raps the song I wrote and performed for her to her sister, with scary-accurate remembrance. Then we call each of our moms to share the news.

More screaming happens.

After what has surely been the death to my eardrums, Bryn clicks end and I snatch her phone, shoving it in my bathrobe (don't knock it until you try wearing one). "No more phones. I want you all to myself."

Bryn stands and saunters over to me. She sits on my lap and holds my face between her palms, hovering her lips just above mine. "And what if I want *you* all to myself?"

I grip her thigh and circle her waist, smiling against her mouth. "All you have to do is ask."

I close the distance between our mouths and kiss her completely. I've never wanted her more than at this moment. Together. Forever. Her and me. Me and her.

When you know, you know.

The End

AFTERWORD

Does it have to be over already? I loved every part of writing Rex and Bryn's story. Like all of my characters, they became real people and real friends throughout the process. I hope you enjoyed reading about their love story.

Thank you to my amazing critique partners and beta readers who have made through yet another book with me. Katie, Janna, Jenessa, Erica, Samuel, René, and Haley. You have all shaped my writing and storytelling in the most intimate ways. Thank you for your comments, suggestions, and encouragement to continue doing what I love and crafting this story.

To Tracey for stepping in to help me edit and proofread this book. You have molded me into a better writer one action beat and comma at a time. I appreciate you all the more for it! Thank you for taking the time to read and provide feedback.

This book is dedicated to a couple of amazing people. First, my husband, Samuel. You shared so much of your travel knowledge and experiences with me, talking through many potential awkward encounters, which helped shape this story. No thanks to your extensive travel schedule and the impressive off-the-wall situations you run up against.

My best friend, Katie—you have been by my side and making me laugh since we were young. We've had plenty of our own airport experiences to look back on and laugh about. There are truly so many and they inspired bits of this story in more ways than one. I can always count on you to put a smile on my face, so I wanted to deliver the same to you. I love you, dear friend!

Lastly, to my readers. I wrote this for you to laugh, smile, and swoon. If you are interested in seeing my inspiration for some of the characters, scenes, outfits, etc. discussed in this book, you can find me on Pinterest @authorchristinahill.

I also love connecting with readers on Instagram and TikTok: @authorchristinahill. If you loved the book, please consider writing a review on Amazon and GoodReads. This is such a tangible way to help authors and I'd be forever grateful!

With all of my love,
Christina

ABOUT THE AUTHOR

Christina is a lover of love who has been writing stories in her head since middle school. She also holds the titles of 'mom' and 'babe' and lives in Montana with her four children, husband, and cat.

When Christina isn't reading or writing, she is wrangling her kiddos, homeschooling, taking baths, baking, or watching **PBS**.

For more information or to sign up for my newsletter, visit www.authorchristinahill.com.

Love at First Flight | Christina Hill

Made in the USA
Columbia, SC
30 December 2022